# REDEMPTION
## BY
## DEFAULT

# ALSO BY

---

## FICTION
*A Killing at Early Dawn*
*Redemption By Default*
*SinSation*
*Dinner With Lexie (A short story)*
*The Silent Syringe (A short story)*
*The Queen's Quest (A short story)*
*ALL-IN (A short story)*
*The Good Daughter (A short story)*
*Unfinished Business (short film)*

---

## NONFICTION
*Letting Him Go When He Cheats*
*The Treasured Coloring Book Collection For Toddlers*

# REDEMPTION
## BY
## DEFAULT

### KATHRYN McGRADY

VISION K. BOOKS

# REDEMPTION BY DEFAULT

# CHAPTER 1

Judge's Bar was hidden in plain sight, nestled beneath the grimy streets of Joliet, Illinois. From above, it appeared nondescript—just another watering hole, unremarkable among the city's neon lights and crumbling brick facades. But the basement room beneath it told a different story. Thick cigarette smoke hovered near the low ceiling like a storm cloud, dim lamps struggling to break through the haze, casting shadows that danced in sync with drunken laughter. The air carried a tang of spilled whiskey and stale sweat.

Tables were scattered around the cramped space, each hosting an intense game of poker. Waitresses maneuvered through the crowd, balancing trays with practiced hands. Their scanty outfits drew lingering gazes, whispers, and occasional grasps. It was the kind of place where the line between pleasure and trouble blurred—and where luck was as fickle as the clientele.

Brad Morgan sat at one of the center tables, a stark contrast to his surroundings. At twenty-eight, his crisp white shirt and his knotted tie, perfect by anyone's standard, suggested he'd stepped straight from a corner office, not a seedy gambling den. His hair, impeccably groomed as if straight out of a men's fashion magazine, reflected the bar's dim lights like polished ebony. But appearances were deceiving. Though his outer attire was composed, beneath the calm facade brewed an anxious determination.

Brad studied his cards. The corners of his mouth curled upward in a faint, confident smile. His voice, smooth yet firm, cut through the cacophony around him.

"I'll raise a thousand," Brad said, pushing a neat stack of chips across the betting line.

The gambler to Brad's immediate left shook his head in resignation. "I fold."

The second gambler hesitated for a few moments before tossing his chips forward. "Match a thousand," he said, his voice gritty, eyes narrowed.

The third gambler, a grizzled veteran with eyes sharp enough to pierce steel, leaned forward, his smile sharp and predatory. "I'll raise two thousand," he said, sliding his stack forward. The chips clicked as they joined the growing pot.

Brad's smile widened as he eyed his opponent. But before the showdown could continue, a loud, aggressive bang echoed from the steel door at the far side of the room, startling everyone into silence. The laughter ceased. Cigarettes hovered motionless between fingers, drinks suspended halfway to mouths.

Into the sudden quiet stepped Big Rob. His hulking figure filled the doorway, face crisscrossed by scars that marked him unmistakably as someone who had tasted—and dealt—violence. A wide-brimmed hat obscured his eyes, and his large overcoat barely concealed his bulky frame. He moved with slow deliberation to a small table in the corner, the heels of his shoes echoing against the concrete floor.

Brad's stomach knotted, the blood draining from his face as Big Rob took his seat. The cards in Brad's hand felt like lead weights. He shifted uncomfortably, pulse quickening, eyes flickering toward Big Rob.

A waitress approached Big Rob, her stride sultry, voice low and inviting. "Sweetheart, what'll it be tonight?"

Big Rob gave her a slow, appraising glance before responding. "Rusty Nail," he said, his voice as coarse as sandpaper.

She tilted her hips. "You can get more than that... just sayin'."

Ignoring the suggestive invitation, Big Rob's gaze is fixed on Brad's table. Brad swallowed hard, forcing himself back to the game. Yet his hands began to shake, sweat forming beads that rolled down his temples. He reached for his glass of scotch, swallowing a large gulp to steady his nerves. It didn't help.

Heart pounding, Brad revealed his hand, his voice trembling. "Four of a kind."

But the seasoned gambler across from him leaned back, laying his cards down with a wicked grin. "Straight flush."

Brad stared numbly, watching helplessly as the winner collected the pile of cash, stuffing it into a leather murse. Big Rob rose from his corner table and approached the table. Brad didn't notice. Each step deliberate and measured. The air grew colder, heavier with each stride.

Big Rob stopped directly beside the winner, his presence suffocating. "You payin' me, right?" His words dripped menace, leaving no room for misunderstanding.

The gambler hesitated, stammering. "Next game, Rob. I—I can't right now—"

With terrifying speed, Big Rob drew a Beretta 92FS from beneath his overcoat, firing three precise shots into the gambler's head. Each gunshot echoed like thunder, blood spraying across the green felt, chips scattering like broken glass. The gambler slumped, his life gone, the murse slipping from his fingers and dropping to the floor.

Silence filled the room. Fear froze everyone in place as Big Rob scooped up his owed cash, leaving the remainder untouched. He turned toward Brad, his cold, unflinching gaze locking onto Brad's terrified eyes.

"You're next," Big Rob growled, the promise clear and chilling.

Without another word, Big Rob reached across the blood-spattered table, took an unfinished glass of whiskey, tossed it back in one swift motion, and exited the room, leaving behind an oppressive silence punctuated by the dripping of blood onto the concrete floor.

Brad's chest tightened. Panic surged through his veins. Without thought or dignity, he shoved his chair backward, almost knocking it over as he bolted from the table. Stumbling through the smoke and shadows, he dashed toward the men's room, desperate to escape the stares, desperate to escape the brutal reality he'd just witnessed.

Brad burst into the men's room, letting the heavy wooden door slam shut behind him. His breath came in ragged gasps, each inhale stabbing at his chest. The sterile brightness of the restroom lighting stood in harsh contrast to the murky, smoke-choked den he'd fled moments earlier. The sudden clarity felt cruel, illuminating every terrified line etched across his pale, sweat-drenched face.

Brad clawed at his tie, fingers trembling as he yanked the knot loose. The tie, perfect moments before, now felt like a noose around his neck, suffocating him. His breath grew shallow and frantic, stomach roiling with nauseating force. He staggered forward, bracing himself against the cold porcelain basin as waves of dizziness crashed through him.

He barely had time to lean over before sickness surged violently upward, forcing its bitter, acidic taste from deep within his stomach. Brad retched into the sink, gripping its edges so hard his knuckles turned white. Sweat mingled with tears at the corners of his eyes, dripping down his face, his chest heaving until there was nothing left but emptiness.

He lifted his head, blinking away the blur of nausea. His gaze met the reflection in the cracked mirror above the sink, and what stared back made him recoil.

Gone was the self-assured, polished salesman he'd always tried so hard to portray. Instead, a hollow-eyed stranger stood before him, face pale, gaunt, etched in fear—a man whose confidence had been shattered by reality. Brad's heart sank, an icy dread settled in his chest, and he didn't recognize himself anymore. He grimaced, disgusted and ashamed, desperately wishing away the trembling figure he'd become.

He reached up weakly, dragging the back of his hand across his lips, trying to wipe away the taste of bile and humiliation. Brad stared into the mirror once more, searching in vain for the man he'd been.

But the mirror reflected a man full of fear.

# CHAPTER 2

B rad sat slumped on his worn, sagging sofa, surrounded by shadows more than usual tonight. The television screen, bright in the darkened living room, displayed the iconic logo from "Man of Steel," its red and gold emblem spanning the entire screen. He watched Superman's image flicker and shift, yet he felt disconnected—unable to find the usual comfort or escape he craved. His fascination with Superman was an irony not lost on him; he admired an indestructible hero yet struggled with his own self-destructive addictions.

On the cluttered coffee table before him sat a half-empty bottle of Johnnie Walker Scotch, its amber liquid catching occasional flickers of blue TV light, shimmering invitingly. Beside it lay a crumpled letter—a grim reminder he'd tried and failed to ignore all evening. Brad reached forward sluggishly, fingers closing around the smooth neck of the bottle. He lifted it to his lips, savoring the fiery burn sliding down his throat, numbing his thoughts just a little more. He placed the bottle back down and eyed the crumpled letter warily.

With a resigned sigh, Brad picked it up and smoothed its creases. His eyes flickered over the formal, emotionless words typed in bold black ink.

"NOTICE OF INTENT TO FORECLOSE."

His heart sank as he scanned further:

*Dear Mr. Morgan,You are hereby notified that the undersigned intends to foreclose under provision of that certain Agreement executed by you on the 20th of June 2015, whereby certain property...*

He took another long pull from the bottle—and that's when the knock came.

Not a polite one. Not a timid knock. Not one he was expecting.

Three sharp raps. The kind that split silence and made the hair rise on the back of your neck.

Brad froze. The bottle hovered halfway to his lips.

Another knock. Harder.

And then—something slid under the door.

Not a bill. Not a flyer. A photograph.

He stared at it for a long moment before daring to pick it up.

It was a picture of his wife.

She stood in profile at a gas station, hand resting a on her round stomach.

Scrawled across the back, in thick, slanted ink:

*"She's still breathing. For now."*

His breath caught. The bottle slipped from his fingers and shattered on the hardwood, but he barely flinched. All the noise in the room—the TV, the wind outside, his heartbeat—vanished under the weight of that one sentence.

She was pregnant. Someone knew. And worse—someone was watching.

Brad's jaw clenched, anger and self-loathing twisting his gut into a hard knot. His breathing grew uneven as reality tightened its relentless grip around him. He crumpled the picture, furious at the helplessness it represented, and flung it toward the nearby wastebasket. It bounced off the rim, landing on the carpet. Another failure.

Brad closed his eyes and tilted his head back against the sofa's faded cushions. He stared at Superman, soaring across the screen, feeling betrayed by his own misguided hopes.

A sudden, thunderous bang shattered the oppressive silence from outside. Brad leaped up, his heart racing. Pounding. He glanced toward the door, paranoia gripping him like cold hands. Gathering his courage, he approached the front door and pulled back the curtain, peering out into the night.

A car had jumped the curb, the front wheels plowing through his trash can, scattering garbage across his driveway. The driver, intoxicated, struggled to straighten the vehicle before lurching down the street. Brad exhaled, shoulders sagging with relief. He stepped outside, shivering in the chilly night air.

Brad walked toward the curb, bending to gather the scattered garbage. As he set the dented trash can upright, a strange feeling prickled at the back of his neck—the sensation of being watched. Straightening, he glanced down the dark street.

Across the way, a black van idled, headlights piercing through the shadows, engine humming with menace. Brad squinted, breath catching. Before he could react, the van surged forward, roaring down the street and vanishing into the night.

Brad swallowed hard, heart pounding. He shook his head, muttering to himself, dismissing the paranoia. Turning back toward his house, he hurried inside, closing the door firmly behind him.

Yet as he stepped back into his living room, another noise startled him—a dull *thud* from within the house. He spun around, pulse hammering at his temples. His eyes darted around, searching for any sign of an intruder.

The sound had come from the hallway closet.

Brad approached, fists clenched, nerves fraying as dread pooled in his gut. Each step louder than the last, echoing ominously in his ears. Reaching out with shaking fingers, he grasped the knob, took a deep breath, and yanked the closet door open.

Inside, a thick hardcover book lay on the floor, it had fallen from its shelf. Nothing more.

Brad stared at the book, relief washing through him so intensely he felt faint. He bent forward, bracing a trembling hand on the doorframe. Another false alarm, another close call that left him even more shaken. Closing the closet, he leaned against it, eyes closed, wishing more than ever for strength he knew he did not possess.

# CHAPTER 3

The shrill, relentless beeping of the alarm clock jolted Brad awake, piercing through the veil of his sleep like needles against his brain. Groaning he reached across Mary's sleeping form to silence the noise. As the room sank back into peaceful stillness, he glanced at Mary's slender figure lying next to him, her dark hair sprawled across the pillow. In the soft morning light, she looked peaceful, untouched by their troubles, like the girl he'd fallen for years ago.

Brad slid closer, wrapping his arm around her waist. He pressed his lips against her shoulder, breathing in her familiar warmth.

"I set the alarm for an extra thirty minutes," Brad murmured into her ear. His voice held a playful warmth, a rare moment of lightness amid their increasing strain. "Don't you want to take advantage of me?"

Mary stirred, smiling as she opened her eyes and turned to face him. Her expression was teasing, a gentle spark flickering despite the fatigue etched beneath her eyes.

"Oh, absolutely," she whispered, tracing her fingers along his chest. "But what'll we do for the remaining twenty-eight minutes?"

Brad chuckled, his pride bruised but his spirit lighter at her playful dig. His eyes sparked. "You'll pay for that," he said, pulling her closer into his arms. "Come here, woman."

Mary laughed as Brad's lips met hers, the worries of their world forgotten in their embrace. For that short, fleeting moment, they reclaimed their intimacy—connecting desperately, and defiantly, as if their passion alone could erase their troubles.

Later, in the cool brightness of their small kitchen, Brad sat at the table, nursing a cup of coffee while flipping through the morning newspaper. Sunlight poured through the window, illuminating the room with a questionable optimistic glow, but it did nothing to soothe Brad's tension. Across from him, Mary picked at her breakfast, occasionally sipping her orange juice, eyes fixed on Brad's distracted expression.

Mary broke the heavy silence. Her voice, though quiet, carried a firm edge. "The bank is trying to foreclose, Brad. Like it or not, I'm pregnant, and we can't afford to lose this house."

Brad stiffened at her words, jaw tightening as he folded the newspaper, setting it down on the table. He forced his voice calm, though irritation simmered just beneath the surface. "We won't lose the house. I promise."

Mary's eyes darkened, her expression growing weary with skepticism. "You promised no more gambling, too," she reminded. Her tone was patient, but frustration flickered behind her gentle composure.

"I'll get the money," Brad replied, averting her gaze. "Don't worry about it."

Mary leaned forward, desperation edging into her voice. "We have counseling this morning, Brad. Remember?"

Brad scowled, bitterness twisting his lips. "That money would be better spent on our real bills, Mary. Not some shrink."

"Therapy is our last chance," Mary insisted, her voice quivering with restrained emotion. "I need you to work with me on this. I can't do it alone."

Brad's eyes flashed, his patience unraveling. He stood his ground, meeting her pleading gaze without flinching. "I won't be there, Mary. No more counseling. I'm done."

Mary's face fell visibly, hurt and disbelief clouding her eyes. Her voice trembled as she fought back tears. "Then how do we make this work, Brad? You can't just refuse to be a father."

Brad felt the pressure of his frustration explode within him, harsh words tumbling out before he could stop them. Mimicking her tone cruelly, he snapped, "You can't do this, you can't do that, you this and you that. Stop blaming me for this! You're the one who decided to get pregnant. It's what you wanted, Mary—so deal with it!"

Mary recoiled, the sting of his words hitting her like a physical blow. Brad immediately regretted the harshness, but pride held him silent. He reached back for the newspaper, snapping it open, hiding his face behind its pages like a shield.

Mary stared at her untouched plate, her appetite now completely gone. The room filled with a thick, oppressive silence, each second stretching between them, driving the wedge deeper.

Mary lifted her fork once, hesitated, and then set it down again with a soft clink that sounded far louder than it should have in the silence. Her hand lingered near the handle, fingers curling, uncurling, as though waiting for a new conversation that would never come.

Across the table, Brad made no effort to lower the paper. She could only see the edge of it, rising and falling with his breath, his presence reduced to a wall of printed words and stubbornness.

She stared at her plate, a smear of jelly, the corner of uneaten toast, the curve of her reflection in the rim of her coffee mug. The room felt too small. The air was heavy with everything he wouldn't say, and everything she was too tired to beg for again.

"I don't want to do this alone," she whispered, not expecting a response. She didn't get one.

Mary pushed her plate away. The legs of her chair scraped against the floor as she stood, slow and deliberate. For a moment, she hovered there, fingers resting on the back of the chair. She looked at the shape behind the newspaper.

"You think this is all just about therapy? About sitting in some office and pretending to listen? It's not." Her voice shook, but she didn't lower it. "This is about you disappearing while I'm standing right in front of you. About how I can scream inside this house, and you won't even flinch."

The paper didn't move.

Mary's mouth trembled, and she pressed her lips together until the urge to cry passed. "You didn't even ask if I was okay. You just told me to deal with it. Like this pregnancy is a problem you never wanted—but I get to live with it. Alone."

She waited again. Nothing. The silence now wasn't passive. It was punishment.

Her hands fell to her sides.

"When our son asks me one day why his father couldn't show up, I want to have something better to tell him than 'he didn't feel like trying.'" Her voice cracked, the words thudding into the quiet like dropped stones. "You may be done, Brad—but I'm not."

She turned and walked toward the hallway.

At the edge of the kitchen, she paused and glanced over her shoulder, hoping—foolishly—that the paper would lower, that he'd look at her, say her name, say anything at all.

But Brad remained motionless, hidden.

Mary left the room, her footsteps soft and steady down the hallway, even as her heart beat a funeral rhythm in her chest.

Behind her, the newspaper rustled—but not out of remorse.

Only to turn the page.

# CHAPTER 4

The Hamilton Haines Insurance office buzzed with constant chatter. Phones rang relentlessly, blending into an ambient hum of persuasion and charm. Insurance representatives perched at desks and cubicles spun practiced lines, assuring clients about protection, safety, and stability—ironic promises given the lives some of them actually led.

Brad Morgan sat tucked away in a cubicle toward the back, hidden from view, his computer monitor casting a pale blue glow across his tired face. He'd long since lost interest in the monotony of sales calls. Instead, his screen displayed scenes from an animated Superman film. Brad stared at his hero, whose effortless strength and integrity mocked Brad's own struggles.

"Superman!" boomed a familiar voice, accompanied by the firm tap of knuckles against Brad's cluttered desk.

Brad jerked upright in startled panic. "Shit!" he blurted, clicking his mouse, closing the animated film, hoping his boss didn't see his screen.

His boss, Mr. Riley—a man in his mid-sixties whose thinning gray hair and warm eyes gave him an air of patient affability—smiled knowingly but said nothing more. He chuckled and continued his casual stroll toward his office, unbothered by Brad's distraction.

Heart pounding, Brad shook off his embarrassment and returned to his monitor. He switched screens, calling up client profiles, returning to the drudgery of his job. Without enthusiasm, he pressed a button on his headset and began his rehearsed pitch.

"Good afternoon, sir, this is—"

"I'm a woman, not a man!" snapped an irritated voice.

Brad winced, glancing at the client's name on his monitor: "Taylor Kennedy." He grimaced inwardly, cursing himself.

"My apologies, Ms. Kennedy," he sprung back. "This is Brad Morgan with Hamilton Haines Insurance, and we're offering—"

A sharp click sounded in his ear. She'd hung up. Brad exhaled, slouching back in his chair. But before he could process his frustration, his desk phone rang. Removing his headset, he lifted the receiver, bracing himself for more annoyance.

"Brad," came the receptionist's crisp voice. "You have an urgent call on line two."

He frowned. With a deep breath, he punched the blinking line.

"This is Brad Morgan. How may I help you?"

A low, threatening filled his ear, sending a cold shiver down his spine. "You can help me by paying me back my money, damn it! Before I stop asking nicely."

Brad's stomach tightened with fear. Glancing around the bustling office, he dropped his voice to a whisper. "I'll get the money, Big Rob. I just need a few more days. I'll pay extra interest."

Big Rob's bitter laugh grated through the receiver. "Of course, you will—if you live long enough." His voice grew soft. "Let me put this in terms even you'll understand...all bets are off."

The line went dead.

Brad hung up, heart racing. Sweat prickled at the back of his neck as fear tightened its grip. Glancing across the room, his eyes settled on Dave Thompson's cubicle. Dave, jovial and perpetually sporting his trademark hat, was Brad's only real friend at the office.

Brad rose, crossing the office and leaning into Dave's workspace. "Dave, I need—"

Dave's phone rang, cutting Brad off. Dave picked it up, signaling Brad to wait. Brad sighed, his anxiety growing by the second.

"Your wife on line three," said the receptionist's polite voice.

"Thanks," Dave replied, clicking the line. His face brightened. "Hello, Lindsey."

But Dave's smile faded as Brad watched him listen to his wife's curt instructions. "I was on my own last night, remember?" Dave muttered.

Brad heard the faint, irritated response from the receiver. "Grow up... I have to work. Everything's not about you."

Dave lowered the phone, staring at it as if he were wounded. Tension filled his jaw as he ended the call. His eyes darkened before he turned back toward Brad, forcing himself to smile.

"Hey, man, you missed another great card game last night. I picked up ten grand."

Brad shook his head, his voice bitter. "I've got no money for gambling right now, Dave. Hell, gambling's why my life is so screwed up."

His friend's smile faded, and Brad leaned in closer, voice barely above a whisper. "Big Rob's threatening to kill me."

Dave's eyes widened with sudden alarm. "The loan shark?"

Brad nodded. "I borrowed money. A lot of money."

Dave hesitated, uncomfortable. "So... what's your plan?"

Brad's voice grew quiet, desperate. "I was hoping you had some ideas."

Dave shook his head, attempting humor to hide his unease. "Nope. Never had a loan shark after me. My wife looks like one, though—and she's definitely out to kill me." His weak laugh faded when Brad didn't react. Dave leaned forward earnestly. "All jokes aside—what about cashing in your policy?"

Brad shook his head miserably. "Wouldn't even come close."

Dave stared incredulously. "You're telling me you're underinsured? Selling insurance is literally your job."

Brad's eyes hardened, defensive. "It's complicated, Dave."

"Oh, right," Dave scoffed, irritated. "Your life's always so much more complicated than mine."

Brad recoiled. "That's not what I meant."

But Dave had already turned away. Brad, feeling utterly defeated, retreated back to his cubicle.

Watching Brad leave, Dave hesitated; he had an idea. He picked up the phone and dialed. "Hey, I need a serious favor," he whispered. "How can I help?" answered a female voice on the other end.

———◆○◆———

Brad paced in the men's room, feeling trapped by the confines of white tiled walls and harsh fluorescent lights. Anxiety churned through him. The door swung open, and Dave stepped in, slapping Brad firmly on the back.

"We should hit Harrah's tonight. I feel lucky."

Brad gave a weary sigh. "You're just going because Lindsey's MIA again."

Dave shrugged, defensive. "This isn't about Lindsey."

"Your story," Brad said flatly. "I can't tonight."

"How can you afford not to?" Dave pressed eagerly. "You need cash, right? Think about what a win tonight could mean—a down payment on a sports car, man!"

"And if you lose?" Brad challenged darkly.

Dave slipped into a stall, voice echoing from within. "Losing's part of the allure, my friend. There's always risk."

Brad leaned against the sink, staring into the mirror. "I lose more than I win. I just need one big score. One."

Dave emerged, washing his hands casually, adjusting his hat with practiced ease. "You might have to settle for a lot of smaller wins, Brad. We're in Joliet—not Vegas."

Dave paused at the door, glancing back seriously. "Make up an excuse to the old lady. You don't want to miss tonight's game."

He left Brad alone in oppressive silence. Frustration exploded through Brad, and without thinking, he punched the mirror hard, glass cracking and splintering around his fist. Blood dripped onto porcelain, mingling with shards of broken reflection.

He stared numbly, feeling more broken than the mirror.

<hr />

Brad sat back down at his cluttered desk, sliding his headset into place with a weary sigh. He stared at the blinking cursor on his screen, mentally bracing himself for the next difficult conversation.

With practiced ease, he tapped a button, connecting to another client.

"Hello, Mrs. Brennan," Brad began, forcing his voice into a soothing, professional cadence. "This is Brad Morgan at Hamilton Haines Insurance. I'm calling regarding the premiums due on your policy."

A brittle, hesitant voice responded. The voice came through like a whisper, weighed down by the strain of age and worry. "I can't send that payment until the first of the month."

Brad closed his eyes, empathy clashing with necessity. "Unfortunately, Mrs. Brennan, your policy will expire before then. I truly don't want to see that happen to you." He paused, swallowing back a lump of guilt. "Perhaps you might borrow from a friend, just temporarily, and repay them on the first—"

"I do not borrow money from friends," Mrs. Brennan interjected, her voice trembling.

Brad winced, rubbing a weary hand over his face. "I understand, ma'am. It was only a suggestion. I would hate for you to lose your policy. A lapse in insurance coverage can be devastating. We do accept credit cards if—"

"My husband will be home soon," she cut in. "I'll discuss this with him and call you back. Goodbye, Mr. Morgan."

Brad exhaled, resigning himself. "Goodbye, Mrs. Brennan."

The call disconnected, leaving him listening to the soft static in the empty line. He removed his headset, feeling the familiar pang of defeat. Leaning forward, he stared down at the insurance papers strewn across his desk.

His eyes caught the stark words printed in cold, bold letters:

**TERM LIFE INSURANCE POLICY***Mr. Brennan, age 85, and Mrs. Brennan, age 80.Policy issued on 7/20/1990.TO BE CANCELLED 7/20/2020 IF UNPAID.*

The words blurred, growing distant as Brad's thoughts drifted into the past.

---

Rain fell in heavy, relentless sheets, battering the mournful gathering in the cemetery. Brad was no older than eight, small and frightened, clutching his father's large, calloused hand. Tears mingled with raindrops on his cheeks as he watched men lower his mother's cheaply made wooden casket into the muddy grave.

"I couldn't afford to send her off properly," Walter Morgan whispered, his voice choked with grief and shame.

Brad's Aunt Mildred stood beside them, her umbrella shaking in her trembling hands. She placed a gentle hand on Walter's shoulder, her voice soft but pointed. "What about the life insurance policy? Sarah told me you purchased one."

Walter's shoulders hunched further under the weight of guilt. "The policy was canceled two months ago for non-payment. We never reinstated it. There just wasn't enough money for basic needs—let alone life insurance."

Before anyone could respond, a sudden, splintering crash echoed through the cemetery, cutting through the sound of the storm. Brad's heart stopped. His mother's casket had slipped, striking the bottom of the grave, splintering apart as everyone stared at it in stunned horror. Pieces of wood fell away, revealing glimpses of the stark white fabric inside.

Walter dropped to his knees, rain pelting his bowed head as his anguished sobs echoed across the cemetery. "My God, what have I done?" he cried, voice broken beyond repair.

Terrified and confused, young Brad turned to his aunt, clinging to her skirt, burying his face in its folds.. His small body shook as he cried, haunted forever by the image of his father broken, defeated, and consumed by regret.

———◆○◆———

Brad blinked, snapping back to reality. A cold, sickening dread churned in his gut, guilt, and sorrow from the past mingling with his current desperation. Without further hesitation, he opened the top drawer of his desk and retrieved a worn rubber stamp marked clearly with the word "PAID."

With deliberate firmness, Brad pressed it onto the Brennans' insurance paperwork. The bold red letters stared defiantly back at him:

**PAID**

Brad exhaled deeply, leaning back in his chair, the weight of his decision heavy but strangely liberating. The gesture wouldn't solve all his problems, but for the moment, at least, he had eased the ghosts of his past.

# CHAPTER 5

Rain hammered the pavement as Brad stepped outside his modest family home, ducking his head to shield his face from the downpour. The morning sky was heavy and gray, matching the leaden weight in his chest. He hurried toward his silver Sebring parked curbside, shoes splashing through puddles that mirrored the dark clouds above.

As Brad reached for the car door, a cold prickle traveled up his spine, halting him mid-motion. Across the street, shadowed by the gloomy weather, sat the black van he'd come to fear, still in the spot he'd seen several times before. His heart lurched, hammering against his ribs, as paranoia tightened its grip.

Brad glanced around, eyes darting to neighboring houses, searching for anything out of place, anything that might indicate immediate danger. Nothing appeared unusual except that damned black van, silent and menacing, lingering like an unspoken threat.

Swallowing hard, he forced himself into the Sebring and slammed the door shut. Rain pounded against the windshield as he twisted around, checking beneath the steering wheel, rifling through the glove compartment, peering into the backseat. However, he had no idea what danger he expected to find. His breathing erratic, he jammed the keys into the ignition and fired up the engine.

With one final anxious glance, he pulled away from the curb, missing the subtle flash of headlights from the black van as it eased away from its parking spot behind him.

Inside the Sebring, Brad tried to steady his nerves by blasting music, the heavy bass vibrating through the car seat. Yet anxiety refused to ease its hold. He glanced up into his rearview mirror. His pulse quickened when he spotted the unmistakable shape of the black van trailing him, headlights blazing in the gray mist of rain.

"Dammit," Brad whispered through clenched teeth, his hands tightening around the wheel.

After another anxious mile, Brad glanced again. The black van was closer now, stalking him like a predator closing in on wounded prey. Brad's heartbeat surged, adrenaline spiking through his veins as fear turned into panic.

Without warning, the black van accelerated, racing up alongside his Sebring. Brad barely had time to register its proximity before the van swerved into his lane, slamming against his car with a deafening crunch.

"Shit!" Brad cried, gripping the steering wheel, fighting to keep control as his car skidded dangerously close to the metal guardrail.

Before he could regain composure, the van collided with him again—harder, more aggressively. Brad's Sebring fishtailed on the slick, rain-slicked road, tires screeching and sliding, nearly sending him spinning into oncoming traffic. Sweat streamed down his forehead, stinging his eyes as panic overwhelmed him.

Through blurry vision, Brad spotted a massive Mack truck barreling toward him, headlights blinding, horn blaring. His breath caught in his throat, terror seizing every muscle in his body. In a last desperate bid for survival, he yanked the wheel hard to the right.

His car veered, tires screaming in protest as Brad's Sebring narrowly cleared the path of the truck. The black van, trapped behind him, had no time to adjust. With a deafening, metallic crunch, the massive Mack truck slammed into it, crushing metal and glass as the van exploded into a violent fireball, flames erupting into the gloomy sky.

Shaking, Brad maneuvered his damaged Sebring off the highway, pulling into the parking lot of a small strip shopping center. He stumbled from the vehicle, lungs heaving as shock and adrenaline surged through his trembling limbs.

Within minutes, but what seemed like seconds to Brad, emergency vehicles raced toward the horrific accident, sirens wailing mournfully in the rain. Brad watched, dazed, as police cruisers and fire trucks swarmed around the fiery wreckage, lights flashing blue and red against the gray landscape.

Feeling dizzy, Brad spotted a small establishment at the far end of the strip mall, its neon sign flickering through the rainy haze. Desperate for something to steady his frayed nerves, he staggered toward it.

Inside the small, quiet bar, Brad collapsed onto a stool, hands shaking against the countertop. The bartender hurried toward him, alarmed by his appearance.

"I need a drink... now!" Brad demanded, his voice cracking with desperation.

The bartender moved behind the bar, returning moments later with a clear beverage, which he placed in front of Brad. "Here you go!"

Brad snatched up the glass and threw its contents back in one large gulp—but immediately choked, spewing the liquid across the bar.

"What the hell was that?" he sputtered, coughing.

The bartender gave him a puzzled look. "Water."

Brad stared, his eyes narrowing in disbelief. He grabbed a menu lying nearby, squinting at the bold lettering on the laminated cover:

*Sam's Veggie Bar*

Brad groaned, throwing the menu back onto the counter. "Oh fuck!" he spat, shoving himself away from the bar and storming out into the relentless rain.

The door slammed shut behind him, but the fury followed. Rain lashed his face, soaking his shirt within seconds, but he didn't stop. He didn't even flinch. It almost felt deserved.

A veggie bar.

He'd just poured out his last drop of energy to land at a goddamn kale-and-quinoa smoothie temple in the middle of downtown Joliet. No liquor. No sin. Just water, tofu, and sobriety.

Perfect.

Brad stopped under the awning of a closed pawn shop two doors down and waited for the rain to stop. His hands trembled—not from the cold, but from a throb just beneath the skin. That crawling heat that came when the edge wore off. The same one that had whispered to him in motel rooms, back alleys, and gas station parking lots.

He needed a drink. A real one. Not water. Not pressed cucumber. He needed something to burn him clean or burn him down—either was fine at this point.

Thunder cracked in the distance. The streets were nearly empty, just a few umbrellas bobbing along and headlights cutting swaths of white through the rain.

Brad dug his phone out of his pocket and stared at it. Water dripped down the screen. One missed call. Mary. He swiped it away with his thumb.

The baby. The house. The fight.

He felt like a loaded gun someone else had cocked, just waiting for the wrong moment to go off.

And now, even the city mocked him. He came downtown looking for oblivion and got kale water instead. Somewhere in the back of his skull, his father's voice—Logan's voice—sneered.

# CHAPTER 6

L ater that day, Brad stood at the counter of Joliet Bank & Trust, feeling drained and numb. He approached a teller, forcing a polite smile that felt more like a grimace.

"Good afternoon, sir," the young woman greeted, unaware of the chaos churning inside him.

"Hello," Brad replied, avoiding eye contact. "I need an account balance, please. Brad Morgan."

The teller nodded professionally, tapping at her keyboard. "Certainly, Mr. Morgan. Would that be your checking or savings account?"

But Brad barely heard her. Her words faded, distorted, as his mind drifted, overwhelmed by visions he could not control...

———◆◇◆———

Brad's vision blurred, reality giving way to a surreal nightmare. He saw himself standing in the center of Joliet Bank & Trust, heart racing beneath a heavy gas mask. Dave stood beside him, similarly masked, both gripping intimidating semi-automatic rifles as panicked customers dropped to the floor. The silent alarm flashed, red lights painting the room in terrifying urgency as tellers cowered behind their stations.

The bank teller's polite but firm voice broke through the terrifying image.

"Excuse me, sir, would that be for your checking or savings account?"

Brad snapped back into reality, gasping, as he steadied himself. He could still feel the phantom weight of the rifle in his hands, the claustrophobic grip of the gas mask pressing against his face. Shaking off the lingering fear, he cleared his throat.

"Oh, uh...my savings," he stammered, pulling out his wallet. His fingers trembled as he fumbled to remove his driver's license, sliding it across the polished counter toward the waiting teller.

The young woman behind the counter studied his identification, then turned toward her computer terminal, her fingers moving across the keys. A moment later, she handed Brad a printed receipt, her expression neutral.

"This is your current balance, Mr. Morgan."

Brad stared down at the small slip of paper, the printed figures unbelievable, mocking him.

*Current Balance: $7,000*

Brad shook his head, anxiety rising within him. His mouth grew dry. "This...this can't be right. Could you double-check the balance, please?"

The teller's eyes flicked to him, a faint hint of irritation crossing her face, but she nodded professionally. Once more, her fingers tapped over the keys, eyes narrowing as she studied the screen.

"You made a large withdrawal of thirty thousand on the 3rd of the month, and another fifteen thousand on the 24th." Her voice held a faint edge of impatience as she glanced up again, holding his gaze, "That leaves ten thousand. Would you like a printout of that?"

Brad shifted uneasily, heat rising in his cheeks as shame flooded through him. He felt exposed, humiliated by his financial reck-lessness. He lowered his voice, eyes downcast. "No, that's...not necessary. I need to withdraw five thousand."

The teller's eyes narrowed subtly, but she swiftly counted out the money, handing it across the counter without further com-ment. Brad stuffed the bills hastily into his pocket and turned away, feeling her judgmental stare drilling into his back as he walked toward the exit.

After he left, the teller shook her head, lips pursed in disap-proval. She leaned toward the colleague beside her, muttering, "They always think they have more money than they actually have—but somehow, we're the dummies."

Her coworker nodded, sharing a sympathetic look as they watched Brad disappear through the bank's revolving door, the cycle of recklessness and denial all too familiar.

# CHAPTER 7

The air in the basement gambling room hung thick with smoke, alcohol, and the scent of desperation. Dim lights dangled from low ceilings, casting just enough glow to reveal the shadowed faces hunched over worn, felt-covered tables.Brad sat rigid, tension coiled in his shoulders as he peered at his cards, trying to project confidence while his heart pounded against his ribs.

Across the table sat Dave, his ever-present cigarette dangling between two fingers, a lazy indifference etched into his features. Beside them, two other gamblers—square and easy targets, Brad had thought—studied their cards in silence, brows furrowed in concentration.

Brad looked again at his hand, a flicker of hope sparking inside him. He drew a breath, the adrenaline kicking hard as he slid his chips into the center. His voice came out steady, though a slight edge crept in."I'll raise five hundred."

Gambler One matched him without hesitation. "Match five hundred.""Match five hundred," echoed Gambler Two, his voice edged with cautious resolve.

Dave took a drag, exhaled smoke through his nose, then flicked his cards onto the table. "I fold," he said, leaning back with a shrug, happy to watch the drama unfold.

The dealer placed the final card for his hand on the table. It was a great card for Brad, so with confidence blossoming, he pushed forward another stack.

"I'll raise a thousand."

Gambler Two frowned, then shook his head. "I fold," he muttered, sliding his cards away and reaching for his drink.

Brad grinned, riding the rush. He locked eyes with the last gambler. This had to be his break. But the man leaned in, eyes cool, voice flat as stone."I'll raise five thousand."

Brad paused for a moment. Then he smiled, heart thundering ."Straight flush," he declared, fanning his cards on the table.

The gambler didn't flinch. He laid down his hand with a bored flick of the wrist."Royal flush."

Shock hit Brad like a punch. His jaw clenched as he slammed his fist down with sudden violence, the crushing weight of his defeat settling on his shoulders."That one hurts," he said through gritted teeth. "I need to go home and lick my wounds."

Dave stood, slipping on his jacket. He tapped ashes to the grimy floor."Wait up, Brad. I'll walk you out."

———◦———

Outside, the night air was sharp and cool, offering a stark contrast to the smoky heat of the gambling den. Brad walked beside Dave across the empty parking lot, lost in his thoughts. When they reached Brad's rental car, Brad shook his head, voice tense with frustration. "Man, I just blew five dimes. I had a great hand. I should have won."

Dave took another drag, exhaling smoke into the crisp darkness. "You knew the risk, Brad. You shouldn't gamble money you can't afford to lose."

Brad pivoted, irritation flaring. "Dave, I don't need you to state the obvious. You were betting too."

Dave shrugged, his eyes distant and detached. "Yeah, but I don't give a fuck anymore. I want my wife to leave me. Better if it's her idea, if I'm broke, she will, without a doubt, leave. It's an easy way out—and I get to have some fun along the way."

Brad watched him, concern and confusion mixing within him. Dave continued, as if speaking only to himself. "If I cheat on her, she'll kill me, Brad. I know she will. But she won't kill me if I gamble myself into poverty."

Brad's voice dropped to a desperate whisper, his troubles overtaking Dave's dark humor. "Dave, listen. I'm in deep trouble. I need two hundred thousand dollars."

Dave laughed grimly, a harsh sound in the quiet parking lot. "Don't we all?"

"No," Brad said, pacing the pavement, fingers trembling as he rubbed the back of his neck. "If I don't get it soon, I'm dead. I borrowed a lot last month and lost even more."

Dave observed him, his cigarette forgotten at his side. "You should go to the police, Brad."

Brad shook his head violently, panic flashing through his eyes. "I can't. They know where I live, Dave. They know where I work. I'm screwed. Do you have that kind of money?"

Dave chuckled, shaking his head. "My wife might—if I had an untimely death. But seriously, no. What about the equity in your house?"

Brad's expression darkened with shame. "We took out a second mortgage when Mary got pregnant. I gambled most of that away. Man, I'm so screwed."

Dave tossed his cigarette onto the pavement, crushing it beneath his shoe, eyes narrowing. "Maybe you should try Vegas. Could be your only chance—outside the lottery or robbing a bank."

Brad scoffed, running a hand through his disheveled hair. "Yeah, maybe I'll rob a bank. How hard could that be, right?"

Dave laughed, the sound hollow and forced. "Come on, Brad. Guys like us don't rob banks." Then he grew serious again, placing a hand on Brad's shoulder. "Look, I can maybe scrape fifty thousand together, but that's it. I wish I could do more."

Brad forced a tired smile, feeling gratitude and hopelessness mixing in his chest. "Thanks, Dave. Seriously. I gotta go home. I'll see you tomorrow."

Dave nodded, stepping toward his late-model convertible parked nearby. The engine purred as he drove away, taillights disappearing into the night.

Brad stood alone, exhaustion settling deeply into his bones. He turned at the growl of an engine revving. His heart leaped into his throat as a sedan tore from its parking spot, tires screeching, racing toward him.

"Shit!" Brad shouted, diving instinctively to the side as the vehicle missed him by mere inches, its headlights blazing past in a terrifying blur. He stumbled, breathing raggedly, heart hammering, as the car sped onto the highway, vanishing into darkness.

Brad stood trembling as the rain started again, hitting his shoulders. Death was circling closer, each near-miss pushing him ever deeper into despair. *Who's after him?*

# CHAPTER 8

The fluorescent lights of the insurance office buzzed overhead, a constant reminder of the sterile monotony Brad had come to resent. At his cubicle, a stack of claim forms and policy summaries sat in disorganized chaos. Brad skimmed through them halfheartedly, though his eyes were glazed, his focus lost. Each printed line blurred into the next, drowned out by the dull roar of his anxiety.

Dave strolled toward him, casual as ever, a familiar glint of trouble dancing in his eyes. He stopped beside Brad's desk and leaned in, lowering his voice like he was sharing a secret that had the power to change everything.

"Hey, man," Dave said, "we're going to Vegas. I've got a friend who owes me a favor. Says she can help you out."

Brad looked up, suspicion rising in his chest. "Help me how?" he asked. "What's involved?"

Dave shrugged, trying to keep things light. "She didn't give me the details, but I trust her. If she says she can help, she can help. Do you have another way?"

Brad's heart sank. The thought of Vegas stirred something deep and unsettled in him: memories, mistakes, and the promise he had made to Mary. "I can't go to Vegas," he said, shaking his head. "Mary will... I can't go."

Dave straightened up, exasperation creeping into his voice. "Hey, you need money. She can help you get the money. What is there to think about?"

Brad stared at him. "Have you met my wife?"

Dave laughed. "You're doing this for her, man—for your family. To save your home. She'll understand."

"No," Brad said. "No... she won't."

As if summoned by the tension, Mr. Riley—balding, brisk, and perpetually unimpressed—wandered by. He gestured toward the two men with mock cheer. "Yapping doesn't help my bottom line, gentlemen. Back to work."

They ignored him. Brad tugged at the knot of his tie, loosening it just enough to breathe. His pulse thudded in his temples.

"Gambling is a sore spot for Mary," Brad muttered, as if trying to reason with himself more than Dave. "Vegas... no. Not happening. Can't you go and bring the cash back yourself?"

Dave smirked. "Way ahead of you. I tried. She said no. She needs us both—for a special project."

Brad narrowed his eyes. "A project we know nothing about."

Dave gave a slight, careless shrug. "Any project that gets me away from Lindsey is a good one. She thinks I'm stupid."

Brad blinked. "What?"

"Never mind," Dave muttered, waving the comment off. Then his tone shifted, more serious, more urgent. "This is your way out, Brad. And you know it."

Brad stared down at the papers in front of him, the lines on the forms blurring again. Something clenched inside him—fear, shame, pride. It didn't matter. He shook his head, firmly. "I'm not going to Vegas."

Without another word, he reached for his headset and slid it over his ears, adjusting the mic like armor. He turned back to his monitor, shutting the conversation down completely.

Dave lingered a second longer, watching him, then let out a frustrated sigh. He threw his hands in the air in surrender and walked away, disappearing into the sea of cubicles.

Brad sat still, staring blankly at the screen, the cursor blinking like a silent warning.

The hum of the office buzzed around him—keyboards clacking, phones ringing, the too-cheerful murmur of a team leader trying to boost morale two desks down. The sound filtered in through one ear while the other was half-muted by the headset. It didn't matter what anyone said. He wasn't hearing any of it. Only Dave's voice rang in his ears.

*This is your way out.*

Brad's fingers hovered over the keyboard, unmoving. He tried to refocus, to read the sentence on the screen, but the words scrambled every time he blinked.

Way out of what?

The mortgage? The baby? Mary? Himself?

He glanced toward the cubicle aisle where Dave had disappeared, then turned his gaze to the manila folder still sitting on the edge of his desk—the one Dave had dropped off earlier, full of hotel contacts, airfare discounts, shady connections that didn't ask too many questions. The folder looked harmless. Ordinary. But Brad knew better.

It was a detonator. All he had to do was open it.

He sat back in his chair, the faux-leather cushion creaking beneath him. His eyes drifted to the ceiling, to the fluorescent lights flickering just enough to make him grind his teeth. How long had he been pretending this job was a safety net and not a cage?

His right leg bounced uncontrollably beneath the desk. He slid the mic away from his mouth and muttered under his breath.

"Jesus."

From the next cubicle, someone laughed too loud. The clatter of a dropped stapler broke the rhythm of the room for a moment. Brad shut his eyes and exhaled.

He didn't want to go to Vegas.

He didn't want to stay here, either.

What he wanted—what he actually *wanted*—was a reset button. A new version of himself that didn't start fights at breakfast, didn't lose track of bank balances, didn't look at his wife and feel... nothing but fear.

He reopened his eyes and pushed the folder farther from him, nudging it toward the edge of the desk. It slid an inch, maybe two, but didn't fall.

Just like him.

# CHAPTER 9

C hris's Steak House was buzzing with the late lunch crowd—servers weaved between tables with practiced grace, the clinking of silverware mingling with lively conversation and the rich scent of grilled meat and wine. Amid the chaos sat Mary Morgan and Lindsey Thompson, tucked into a corner booth that offered just enough privacy for the kind of conversation Lindsey had come prepared to have.

Lindsey, elegant in a form-fitting blazer, pushed her salad aside and leaned forward, her voice low but firm. "I'm thinking about leaving Dave."

Mary blinked, fork hovering midair. "Why? What happened?"

Lindsey sighed and lowered her gaze to her untouched plate. "There's someone else. It's been six months now. I didn't want you to judge me—but I need to talk about it. I'm tired of holding it in."

Mary's voice softened with concern. "Does Dave know?"

"No... but he might suspect. I haven't exactly been home much lately."

Mary folded her hands in her lap, the weight of the moment settling between them. "Are you sure you want to end your marriage? You and Dave have been together over ten years."

Lindsey laughed dryly, her expression hardening. "It feels like twenty. There's no passion. No spark. No real connection. I don't even think we like each other anymore."

Mary hesitated. "Have you tried counseling? Brad and I—"

Lindsey waved the idea away. "Counseling won't help. Dave just doesn't get me. He never really has. I'm glad we never had kids. At least I don't have to explain this to anyone else but him."

Mary's eyes dropped to her plate. She poked at a piece of grilled chicken with her fork but made no move to eat it.

Lindsey, noticing the shift in her friend's demeanor, softened her tone. "Oh... but it's not like you and Brad. Brad will come around."

Mary's lips curled into a tight, faint smile. "No worries. It was my choice to have this baby. Brad's lack of interest doesn't change that. I have no regrets."

Lindsey picked up her wine glass and drained it in a single, unflinching gulp. She set it down with a light clink. "When the baby comes, and he holds him—or her—in his arms, he'll fall in love. You'll see. Men are more emotional than women, Mary. They just hide it better... sometimes too well."

She looked down at her plate, pensive. Mary studied her for a moment.

"Are you okay?" she asked.

Lindsey laughed again, this time with a touch of bravado. "I've got a great career. Great sex—with someone who isn't my husband. And a shoe collection Imelda Marcos would rise from the grave to envy. I'm good."

Mary tilted her head unconvinced. "How are you going to tell Dave? You know he puts up this front, but he worships the ground you walk on. This will break his heart."

Before Lindsey could respond, their waiter appeared, a slim, well-groomed man carrying a fresh bottle of wine.

"Would you like some more wine?" he asked, smiling politely.

"Yes, thank you," Lindsey said with a flirty lilt.

The waiter filled her glass and turned to Mary.

"And you, miss?"

Mary hesitated only for a moment. "Absolutely."

Once their glasses were full, the waiter stood poised. "Would there be anything else I can get you ladies?"

"No, we're good," Lindsey replied smoothly.

"Thank you," Mary added.

As the waiter walked away, Lindsey watched him go, her eyes following the sway of his retreating figure.

"Damn," she muttered, to herself. "What an ass on that waiter... my, my, my."

She took another sip of wine, then sighed. "Anywho. I know Dave loves me. I don't want to hurt him but staying married to someone you don't love is just as cruel. I've tried everything. Nothing's changed. Nothing will."

She stared into her wine glass for a long beat. Then, as if admitting it to herself for the first time: "No. Leaving is the only answer. He's incapable of change. It's over."

Mary nodded. "As long as you're sure about what you're doing..."

"I am sure," Lindsey said with conviction. She paused again, then added, "When Dave gets back from Vegas—"

"Dave is going to Vegas?" Mary interrupted, her brow furrowing.

Lindsey looked up. "Brad is going with him. You didn't know?"

Mary froze, her stomach sinking.

"Brad hasn't said a word," she said.

Lindsey's expression fell. "Oh."

The room tilted for a moment. Mary blinked hard, reaching instinctively for her water glass to steady her hand, though she had no intention of drinking from it. Her fingertips trembled against the condensation as she processed what Lindsey had just said.

Vegas.

Brad had mentioned needing "space." He'd sulked at breakfast, picked a fight about counseling, buried himself in his computer. But he hadn't said a word about a trip.

And now, it wasn't just a trip—it was *Vegas*. With Dave.

A tight pressure bloomed in her chest.

She cleared her throat. "Do you know when they're leaving?"

Lindsey shook her head. "Dave just said something about wrapping things up at work first. I didn't get the impression it was planned to the minute. Just... soon."

Mary's thoughts scattered like loose papers in a gust of wind. She tried to make sense of it, tried to fold it neatly into the list of things Brad did that made her feel invisible—but this one hurt in a different way.

He was planning to leave. And he hadn't told her.

Not even a hint.

"Maybe I misunderstood," Lindsey said, the tension in her voice shifting. "I just assumed you knew."

Mary forced a smile. "It's fine," she lied. "You didn't do anything wrong."

But inside, her thoughts pulsed with suspicion. Brad had been hiding something. Again. And not something small. Not something accidental. This was deliberate.

The baby shifted inside her—not a kick, just the quiet pressure of growth—and it brought her back to the moment. She pressed a hand to her stomach protectively and looked out the window of the restaurant at the late afternoon sky, clouds dimming into gold.

"He promised me he'd try," Mary said, more to herself than to Lindsey. "He said he wanted to do better."

Lindsey stayed silent, her gaze lowering to her lap.

Mary knew that look. She'd worn it herself once—back when the truth stopped being surprising and just became inevitable.

# CHAPTER 10

The wind swept across the Morgan backyard with a biting chill that didn't belong to spring. Though the calendar promised late May in Joliet, Illinois, the air whispered of October. The moon hung behind a gauzy curtain of clouds, casting a pale glow over the patio and throwing long, eerie shadows across the lawn.

Brad and Mary sat together on the patio swing, its old chains creaking with each gentle rock. The hush between them wasn't uncomfortable, but it was weighted—filled with everything unspoken. Brad kept his hands folded in his lap, staring out at the darkened yard, while Mary tugged her sweater tighter around her shoulders, the breeze tugging at the edges of her sleeves like unseen fingers.

She shivered. "It's colder than I expected," she murmured.

Brad nodded, his gaze fixed ahead. "The seasons don't know what they're doing anymore."

The wind stirred again, stronger this time, rattling the leaves and sending a dry sigh through the trees lining the fence. Mary leaned into Brad, seeking warmth more from the presence than the heat of his body.

In the thick silence, neither of them noticed the stillness beyond the porch lights—the way the shadows didn't shift naturally, the way the darkness near the hedges didn't quite move with the wind.

A figure stood there.

Motionless. Watching.

From the safety of the trees just beyond the glow of the house, the shadowy figure blended with the night. Eyes fixed on the couple, unmoving. Waiting.

Mary nestled closer to Brad as the swing rocked beneath them, unaware of the silent witness only yards away or that the night had grown darker than it should have.

Brad shifted on the patio swing, the rusty chains groaning under his weight as he turned toward Mary. The wind tousled his hair, chilled his skin, but he barely noticed. He took a breath—deep, deliberate—and broke the silence between them.

"We need to talk."

Mary didn't look at him right away. She stared out into the darkness, arms folded tight around her chest, her breath visible in the cold spring air. "That's a first," she said, her voice clipped.

Brad flinched at her tone but pressed on. "What's the problem, Mary?"

She turned to face him then, eyes sharp. "Vegas? Really? Gambling? Again?"

He sighed. "Lindsey."

Mary's jaw clenched. "She didn't know it was a secret."

"It's not," Brad replied. "I told Dave I wasn't going, and I'm not. Lindsey only got half the story right."

Mary narrowed her eyes. "You know how I feel about gambling."

"Yes," he said, reaching behind her to pull her closer. His hands slid over her arms, rubbing them up and down, trying to warm her. "You've been painfully clear. I'm not going, baby. End of story."

Mary didn't move right away. The swing rocked beneath them. A curl of wind drifted past, lifting the hem of her sweater. "This cold..." she said, to herself, "I don't mind. That rub of yours never gets old."

She gave him a faint smile. A real one—small, but present.

Brad smiled too, the tension in his shoulders loosening just a bit. "C'mon," he said, nodding toward the house. "Let's get inside."

Mary hesitated, then leaned back against his chest, savoring the rare moment of closeness. "I can't remember the last time we sat out here and just... talked. I miss that."

Brad looked down at her, the corners of his mouth softening. He brushed a lock of hair behind her ear, the gesture gentle, reverent. "It's cold," he repeated, though his voice was tender. "Let's go in. Johnnie Walker's waiting for me."

He stood and offered his hand. Mary rose, letting him guide her. Their footsteps echoed against the concrete as they crossed the patio and approached the back door of the house.

"Okay, Mr. Morgan," Mary said lightly, "I—"

She never finished the sentence.

The door creaked open—and in an instant, chaos erupted.

Two hooded men sprang from the darkness behind them, guns raised, voices sharp and commanding. The barrels gleamed in the porch light.

"Inside. Now!" one of them barked.

Mary screamed, but it was cut short by the shove of a gloved hand against her back. Brad tried to shield her, stepping in front, but the second man drove a gun into his ribs with a brutal jab.

"Move!" the first shooter snarled.

Forced inside at gunpoint, the swing behind them creaked in the wind, still rocking—now empty, still warm. The patio was silent once more. But the night was far from over.

The kitchen lights were still on, casting long shadows across the linoleum floor as Brad and Mary were shoved inside. The wind from the open door howled behind them, but the chill was nothing compared to the icy panic in the room.

"Sit!" barked the first shooter, his face hidden beneath a dark hood. He jabbed his pistol in Mary's direction.

She stumbled toward the kitchen table, her limbs stiff with terror, and collapsed into the nearest chair. Her wide eyes flicked between the two intruders.

Brad hesitated, instincts torn between defending her and staying alive.

Too slow.

The second shooter, taller and more volatile, kicked Brad hard in the ribs. Brad cried out and crumpled to his knees. Then the boot came down again, stomping into his side with brutal force.

Mary screamed.

"Shut the fuck up!" Shooter One snarled, raising his gun toward her head.

She froze, tears spilling over her cheeks, mouth trembling with suppressed sobs.

Shooter Two slung his backpack off his shoulder and set it down on the table with deliberate precision. He unzipped it and pulled out a roll of duct tape, a slender, gleaming knife, and several coils of rope. The tools made a chilling contrast against the clean surface of Mary's white kitchen table.

Without a word, he approached Mary, tore off a strip of duct tape, and pressed it tightly across her mouth. She whimpered as he jerked her arms behind her and cinched them together with the coarse rope.

"Don't you hurt her!" Brad growled, trying to rise.

"What?!" the second shooter snapped, whirling on him. "What are you gonna do?"

He grabbed Brad by the collar, yanked him up, and jammed the cold steel of a revolver against Brad's temple. Brad barely had time to react before the pistol came crashing into his face—again and again. The brutal pistol-whipping sent blood spraying across the floor, his groans muffled by gritted teeth.

"On the floor!" the shooter roared. "Now!"

Brad, dazed and battered, looked for an opening to fight back, to escape—but there was none. He obeyed, slumping to the floor as his vision swam.

Mary watched in horror, bound, and gagged, eyes wide with panic as the second shooter crouched over Brad, brandishing the knife. He ran its sharp edge lightly down Brad's nose, just enough to send a warning.

"Do you have the money?" he hissed.

"I can get it!" Brad choked out, voice weak.

"That tune..." The shooter tilted his head. "Yeah... that one's stuck in my head. Over and over. Real tiring."

From across the room, the first shooter barked, "Hey! We need to get on the road. You're wasting time on this punk."

But Shooter Two didn't move. He turned, irritated, then grabbed his backpack again. He pulled out a small towel, spread it neatly on the floor, and laid out a surgical suture kit with eerie precision.

Brad stared in confusion, trying to sit up. "What are you doing?"

The shooter said nothing. He reached for the duct tape and sealed Brad's mouth shut in one swift motion.

"You know the saying?" He murmured, slipping on a pair of surgical gloves. "This is going to hurt me more than it hurts you. Yeah... that's a lie."

He doused the knife with alcohol. The smell stung Brad's nose even before the cold metal touched his skin.

Then came the pain.

A sharp, agonizing incision cut into Brad's left side. He screamed, but the sound muffled into a pitiful, wet groan beneath the duct tape. Blood pooled, trickling across the floor.

From the backpack, the shooter withdrew a small sandwich bag. Inside was a black, shiny object no bigger than a matchbox fixed with a blinking timer.

With careful precision, he placed the device inside the incision. Brad's body jerked involuntarily.

Then the suturing began—quick, clean, professional. The cut was sewn shut like a stitched seam in a garment. The shooter worked with a surgeon's expertise, and a butcher's detachment.

"Don't get why Big Rob doesn't just shoot him in the head and be done," the shooter muttered as he finished.

"Big Rob's all about the drama," his partner replied from the doorway. "He gets off on this shit."

Brad lay on the floor, barely breathing, sweat pouring from every pore, eyes wide in stunned disbelief.

The first shooter stepped over to Mary and cut the ropes binding her wrists. Without another word, both men turned and fled into the night.

Mary tore the tape from her mouth with shaking fingers, her face streaked with tears. "Brad!" she cried, crawling across the floor to him. She ripped the tape from his face and wrapped her arms around him as he gasped for air.

"I'm sorry, baby," Brad whispered, his voice hoarse and broken. "I'm so sorry."

Mary clutched him tightly. "It's not your fault," she said, though her voice was already cracking.

Then her body spasmed. She bent forward and screamed, a raw, painful cry that ripped from deep within her.

"Mary?!" Brad tried to stand, wincing as pain lanced through his side. "What's wrong? Is it the baby? Let's go. Come on."

He stumbled to his feet, blood dripping beneath his shirt. He staggered toward the hallway closet, threw it open, and grabbed their coats.

Mary pointed at his sutured side, panicked. "What about—what they did to you?"

Brad gave her a shaky smile, full of defiance and despair.

"Man of steel, baby," he whispered. "Man of steel."

# CHAPTER 11

The sterile, fluorescent-lit corridor of Northwestern Memorial Hospital stretched endlessly before Brad, but he kept pacing, back and forth, his footsteps muffled against the polished floor. The pain in his side throbbed, deep, and constant, but he ignored it. His focus was locked on the small window in the door to Mary's room.

Through the glass, he observed her lying in the hospital bed, pale against the crisp white sheets. A monitor beeped in the background. The doctor stood beside her, checking vitals, speaking in a low, measured tone. Brad leaned closer, his breath fogging the glass, anxiety tightening around his chest like a vise.

The door opened, and the doctor stepped into the hallway, clipboard in hand. Brad straightened and pulled his jacket tight, subtly concealing the sutured wound beneath his shirt. He tried to appear composed, but tension radiated from every inch of him.

"Doctor," he said, voice low and urgent. "How's my wife?"

The doctor paused, eyeing him with professional scrutiny. "What happened?"

Brad offered the quickest lie he could manage. "A petty theft. She got upset. That's all. Is she okay? Is the baby okay?"

The doctor studied him for another beat, then nodded. "They're both fine. But she needs to rest—no stress. She was shaken, and with pregnancy, that's never ideal."

Brad exhaled, the weight on his shoulders easing just enough to breathe again. He nodded. "No problem. Thank you. Really—thank you, doctor."

⎯⎯◆⎯⎯

Inside the dim hospital room, machines hummed, and monitors glowed in the low light. The steady rhythm of Mary's heart monitor tapped like a slow metronome, keeping time with the silence that hung between them.

She lay sleeping, her face soft and peaceful despite the terror of the night. Her hair was damp at the temples, and her lips moved with shallow breaths. Brad stepped inside and moved to her bedside. He stooped and kissed her forehead, the warmth of her skin grounding him in a way nothing else had all day.

Then he sank into the chair beside her, letting himself feel the exhaustion. His shoulders slumped forward, and he lowered his head, hands clasped between his knees. The adrenaline had run its course, leaving his limbs heavy, his mind too full of static to think clearly.

For a few moments, he just sat there. The beeping. The drip of an IV. The hush of machines working to keep things steady. It felt wrong somehow—that a room filled with so much life-saving equipment could feel so fragile.

"Brad?"

Her voice was a whisper, barely audible. But it cut through the silence like a bell. He looked up instantly and rose to his feet, moving closer, taking her hand in his.

"Our baby—"

"—is doing fine," he said, already leaning forward, brushing his thumb across her knuckles. "No talking. Just rest."

But Mary's eyes were wide, unfocused, her mind still trapped somewhere in the aftermath.

"What are we going to do?" she asked. "What if they come back?"

Brad's jaw tightened. He hated how her voice sounded—so small, so unsure. Hated even more that he didn't have a clean, honest answer. He gripped her hand tighter. His voice came out firmer now, steadier, filling the corners of the room like armor.

"They won't," he said. "I'll deal with it. But I need you to trust me. Can you do that?"

Mary stared at him, her eyes searching his face—looking past the calm surface, down to the fear he was trying so hard to hide.

She nodded.

Her fingers curled around his hand, holding tightly.

Brad didn't move. He didn't speak again. He just stood there letting her believe he had a plan.

But, the truth was, he had no plan. Big Rob was after him, and he might send his goons again, with no warning. Just shadows now lurking at the edges of their lives, faceless and silent.

And a child on the way.

He turned back to the chair and sat once more, keeping his hand in hers.

He stared at the door.

It had been locked earlier, he was sure of it. But now, in the darkness, he watched the silver handle and waited—just in case.

# CHAPTER 12

From a secluded balcony high above the Vegas Strip, Logan Mulroney stood still as stone. The neon world below buzzed with life—cars flowing like blood through the arteries of the city, lights blinking in hypnotic rhythms, voices rising in waves from tourists who didn't know they were dancing through someone else's scope.

Logan, at forty-six, was the definition of composed elegance. His temples bore streaks of gray that only added to his distinguished aura, while his frame remained lean and athletic—still sharp from years of disciplined training. In his tailored charcoal jacket, he might have passed for a high-end art dealer or the owner of a boutique hotel. The only thing out of place was the black tactical backpack slung over one shoulder—functional, not fashionable.

He raised a pair of binoculars and adjusted the focus with a precise flick of his fingers. Through the magnified lens, two men dined on a rooftop terrace across the boulevard, laughing, gesturing with the careless abandon of men who thought time was still on their side. They tore into thick cuts of steak and clinked their glasses with theatrical flair, as if each bite and sip might be their last.

Logan's phone vibrated against his thigh. He pulled it from his coat pocket. A photo lit up the screen—a headshot of one of the men, paired with a name and a number he didn't need to memorize. He studied it for a beat, eyes cold and unreadable.

With a fluid motion, he crouched down and unzipped the backpack. From within, he withdrew a bottle of Jura scotch. The glass was cool against his palm. He unscrewed the top, tipped it back, and took two long, burning swigs. The taste was peaty and sharp, cutting through the dryness of his mouth. It steadied him, but not too much. He never wanted to be too steady. There had to be a little shake in the soul if you were going to take another man's life.

He returned the bottle to the pack, then opened a long, matte-black rifle case beside him. Inside, nestled like a holy relic, was a massive, custom-built rifle—sleek, heavy, and deadly. He ran a cloth over it once, more from ritual than necessity. Then he stood, cocked it with a smooth, mechanical click, and shouldered it.

His eyes returned to the scope.

The target leaned back in his chair, laughing with a mouth full of half-chewed meat. Perfect.

But just as Logan's finger curled around the trigger, a sudden blur of movement caught his eye.

From the shadows of the open backpack, a gray tabby sprang forward—Snoop, his silent companion in too many missions to count. The cat darted across the balcony and vanished behind a low stone wall.

"Snoop," Logan hissed under his breath, eyes never leaving the scope. "Snoop!"

He took a steadying breath, reacquired the target, adjusted for the breeze—then fired.

The crack of the rifle echoed like distant thunder across the night sky.

Through the scope, he watched the bullet hit. A perfect shot. Dead center. The man's head snapped back, crimson blooming in a grotesque flower across the table. Glass shattered. Forks clattered. Blood ran like spilled wine.

Logan exhaled—but it was cut short by a sound that sliced through the night.

A child's scream.

He jerked the binoculars to his eyes and searched wildly. There—just beside the fallen man—a young boy wailed over the body, clutching at the man's lifeless chest. His sobs rang out even from this distance, tearing through Logan with more force than the recoil of his weapon.

"Shit," Logan muttered. "Shit! Shit!"

He lowered the binoculars, his hands clammy. He wiped his brow with a folded handkerchief, then shoved the binoculars and rifle back into their cases, movements jerky now, less measured. The boy's scream lingered in his ears like a judgment he couldn't scrub clean.

He grabbed the Jura again and took another swig, longer this time, hoping to drown what he couldn't undo. Then he scanned the balcony.

"Snoop," he called. "Snoop!"

He rounded the corner, heart pounding for the first time all night, and found the cat licking its paws near a stone planter, unbothered and feline as ever.

Logan exhaled and scooped him up. Snoop blinked up at him with calm, indifferent eyes.

"Behave," Logan muttered, tucking the cat into the vented chamber of the backpack. "Or we won't make it out of Vegas. Nine lives will only be a fantasy."

He stroked Snoop's back once, zipped the pouch halfway shut, and tightened the pack over his shoulders.

Then, without a sound, Logan disappeared into the shadows—just another ghost retreating from the lights of the Strip.

⊷◉⊷

The morning sun poured through the floor-to-ceiling windows of Logan Mulroney's penthouse, bathing the sleek space in a golden glow. The view was nothing short of breathtaking—an uninterrupted panorama of the city's skyline, glittering like a dream still trying to wake up. But despite its beauty, the apartment felt sterile, like a showroom for a life curated but never lived.

Minimalist furnishings—gray, black, and white—created an ambiance of icy precision. There were no photos. No clutter. No trace of sentiment. Just sharp lines, polished surfaces, and silence.

In the bedroom, Logan moved with his usual efficiency. His walk-in closet was a display of curated luxury: rows of tailored suits in grays, navies, and deep charcoals lined one wall, flanked by shelves of gleaming Salvatore Ferragamo and Bruno Magli shoes, each pair aligned. On the back wall, dozens of hats and ties were organized by color and material, a quiet testament to his obsession with detail.

Without hesitation, he plucked a dark sapphire suit from the rack, paired it with a crisp white shirt, a charcoal tie with silver accents, and a charcoal fedora that gave him an air of old-world elegance.

He turned, then moved to the back wall and slid it aside, revealing a hidden weapons room.

Unlike the clean design of the rest of the apartment, this chamber was unapologetically utilitarian. Rifles, handguns, and knives lined the walls like a museum of violence. The scent of oiled metal and leather lingered in the air. Logan opened a matte black case and retrieved a gleaming .357 Magnum, running his fingers along its barrel before sliding it into the holster on the table. The weight of it felt familiar. Reassuring.

From a row of knives arranged by size and purpose, he selected a small, narrow blade with a polished obsidian handle. A flick of his wrist sent it gliding into a calf holster beneath the hem of his tailored trousers.

When he emerged, Logan was fully armed, meticulously dressed, and prepared to kill.

In the living room, he crossed to the coffee table and lifted the half-empty bottle of Jura scotch. He poured two fingers into a crystal tumbler and took a slow sip, letting the smokey burn slide down his throat like a morning ritual.

Beside the bottle sat a notepad.

He picked it up, eyes scanning the list—names printed in black ink, each one a death sentence waiting to be carried out. Most were already crossed off, lines drawn with such precision they were almost surgical.

INSERT – THE PAD:*Senator Worthen* *Hugo Mintz* *Paul Huntington* ~~*Barry Long*~~ ~~*Evan Gregory*~~

Logan reached for the pen on the table and crossed off *Paul Huntington* with the same cold finality he'd delivered the bullet the night before. The pen clattered back onto the glass.

He dropped the pad and stared blankly at the television. A muted news anchor gestured at a map. Logan didn't hear the words—he didn't need to. The silence in his mind had grown louder over the years.

From outside the window, the faint sound of children playing drifted up from the courtyard below. Laughter echoed between the buildings—innocent, unbothered, alive.

Logan stood and walked to the window, scotch in hand, staring down at the tiny figures racing beneath trees, their voices carried upward by the breeze. For a moment, something unreadable flickered across his face—longing, or perhaps memory.

Snoop, his gray tabby, padded across the floor and brushed against his leg. Logan reached down and scooped the feline into his arms. Snoop purred contentedly as Logan stroked the back of his neck with slow, absent motions.

He stared out at the morning world as if it belonged to someone else.

"One more hit," he whispered, barely audible, "and it's just you and me."

Snoop blinked up at him, and Logan closed his eyes, holding the cat against his chest.

The city kept moving, unaware that death had paused for a breath.

# CHAPTER 13

The morning sun glinted off the mirrored glass exterior of a downtown high-rise, casting shards of light across the polished pavement. A GQ dressed businessman, clad in a tailored pin-stripe suit, clutched a silver briefcase with the urgency of someone late to a meeting that could change his life. He moved toward the waiting elevator, oblivious to the man already inside.

Logan Mulroney stood near the back of the elevator car, a spectral figure of poise and death. His ensemble was flawless—an obsidian three-piece suit with a charcoal tie and a felt hat tilted just so. As always, he was dressed to kill—literally and figuratively. His presence exuded a calculated chill, the kind that made people keep their distance.

The businessman stepped in and offered a polite nod. "Good morning," he said, his voice buoyant, cheerful.

Logan responded with a curt nod, his eyes unreadable behind subtly tinted lenses.

The elevator doors slid shut with a quiet sigh. A brief second passed. Then—

Logan struck.

With the fluid precision of someone who had done this many times before, Logan lunged forward and drew a small blade from beneath his jacket. Before the businessman could utter another word, Logan sliced cleanly across his throat. The man's eyes bulged in shock, and his knees buckled. Blood gushed from the wound like a red ribbon unraveling, splashing against the mirrored walls and pooling on the polished floor.

The briefcase slipped from his grip and hit the ground with a dull metallic thud. Logan caught it with one hand and calmly stepped over the body as the elevator slowed to a stop.

The doors slid open.

An elderly woman stood just outside, her face wrinkled and kind—until her eyes landed on the blood-soaked horror inside. She opened her mouth and unleashed a scream so shrill it echoed off the marble walls of the lobby.

Gasps followed. People turned. A receptionist bolted from behind her desk.

But Logan was already gone.

◄O►

Logan strolled through the chaos like a man on his way to brunch, unfazed and untouched. The briefcase swung at his side. His hat was still in place. He reached the exit doors just as they opened, welcoming him into the morning light.

A sleek black limousine idled at the curb. The driver didn't need a signal. He stepped aside and opened the door.

◄O►

Inside the opulent vehicle, a gray tabby lounged regally on the leather seat as if he owned the vehicle and its contents. Snoop barely flicked an ear as Logan slid in beside him.

Logan set the briefcase on the seat, pulled his backpack onto his lap, and withdrew his cell phone. He thumbed a number from memory and brought it to his ear. His jaw was clenched.

The call connected.

"Yeah," came the gravelly voice of Parker Hart, thick with nicotine and contempt.

Logan's voice was cold and cutting. "Are you trying to fuck me?"

Parker exhaled, the hiss of his cigar audible even over the line. "I prefer three holes, if you know what I mean."

"I said—are you trying to fuck me?"

A pause. Then laughter, low and cruel. "I understand education was an afterthought, but even you can do better than that."

"I could slit your throat in half a second," Logan muttered, his voice barely above a whisper, but lethal all the same.

Parker snorted. "You'd have to slit mine, my brother's, my uncle's, my son's, my nephew's—and my wife's. Trust me, you don't want to mess with my wife. The bitch is crazy."

The line crackled as Parker took another drag. "What is this about? What's the damn problem?"

"Huntington had a son," Logan said. "He was in the restaurant last night."

"So what? You wouldn't have done the hit if you had known?" Parker scoffed.

"I told you my rules going in," Logan said. "I don't make orphans. You knew that."

"Well guess what, Saint Logan?" Parker growled. "Most people have kids."

Logan's grip tightened on the phone. "I shot him in front of his son."

"I don't have time for this bullshit," Parker snapped. "Where's my money?"

The line went dead.

Logan lowered the phone without a word. The weight of silence filled the limo like fog. He looked at the briefcase, its metal surface smeared with a trace of blood.

Snoop stretched and yawned.

Logan reached out and scratched the cat behind the ears, his expression unreadable.

The car rolled forward into the glinting light of the Las Vegas morning, the sins of the city rolling beneath its wheels.

Logan sat motionless, the phone still resting loosely in his palm. He stared through the tinted window, watching the strip come alive—billboards flashing, pedestrians dragging hangovers behind them, neon promises offering redemption with fine print that would destroy you.

He'd seen it all before. A thousand versions of the same lie.

He dropped the phone onto the seat beside him and reached for the briefcase. The metal was still warm from the sun, but under it, he could feel the faint tackiness where the blood had dried. He didn't wipe it off. There was no point.

Purring, Snoop rubbed his head against Logan's arm. Logan glanced down, then gave the cat another slow scratch behind the ears.

"I told you," he murmured. "I don't shoot for money anymore."

Snoop yawned again, as if unimpressed.

Logan leaned back against the leather, one ankle resting over his knee, casual in posture but braced internally. Parker wasn't going to let this slide. Not the insult. And definitely not the missing money.

The thing was—Logan didn't give a damn about Parker's threats. But he knew what men like Parker did when they couldn't get to you.

They found someone close instead.

He reached into his coat and pulled out the wallet of the man he'd shot. A photo fluttered loose as he opened it—a cheap print-out, edges curled, the kind a kid might carry in his backpack.

Father and son. Matching baseball caps. Smiling.

Logan stared at it longer than he meant to. Then he folded it, tucked it neatly back inside, and slipped the wallet into the seat pocket across from him.

He didn't want it. But he couldn't throw it away either.

He looked down at Snoop, now curled into a loaf at his side.

"We're going to have company," he said. "And it won't be polite."

The cat blinked, unimpressed.

Logan reached into the briefcase and lifted the pistol that waited there. The blood was his own this time—a split knuckle from smashing a locked door open earlier. Nothing worth dressing.

He checked the chamber. Full. Clean.

He slid it back into place.

Outside, the Vegas morning widened into full sun, glaring and merciless. Tourists gathered at crosswalks, oblivious. Somewhere, far off, a siren wailed. And somewhere closer, Parker was dialing someone else—someone with less hesitation.

Logan's lips barely moved.

"Let them come."

# CHAPTER 14

Logan sat up, the sheets sliding off his torso, and swung his legs to the side of the bed. The room, awash in soft gray light, offered no comfort. He stared off into the distance, his eyes vacant, his jaw tight. The city beyond the glass stretched endlessly, glittering, and indifferent.

A soft thump drew his attention.

Snoop, his gray tabby, leapt onto the bed with feline grace and padded toward him. Logan's expression softened. He extended his hand and scratched behind the cat's ears, then ran his fingers down its spine. Snoop purred in response, leaning into the touch like he owned the world—and Logan.

With the cat tucked in his arms, Logan stood and padded to the window. The view was staggering—a sprawl of towers and neon humming beneath the rising sun. Vegas, in all its ruthless beauty.

Then came the crash.

A loud, splintering sound shattered the quiet—wood and metal giving way under brute force. Logan's instincts took over. He crouched behind the bedroom door, heart rate slow, eyes sharp. Snoop bolted from his arms and darted under the bed, tail taut with alarm.

Logan smirked. "Chicken-shit," he muttered under his breath.

Footsteps followed. Measured. Soft. A silhouette moved into view—a figure clad in black, a small handgun angled toward the ceiling. The intruder approached the bedroom door, then nudged it open with his foot. Darkness met him.

He stepped in.

Before the intruder could adjust to the low light, Logan struck.

In one swift motion, Logan surged forward and locked his forearm around the man's neck, dragging him backward into a chokehold. The gun dropped with a muffled thug onto the carpet. Logan slammed a heavy punch into the side of the man's head, then paused. Something about the angle of the jaw, the twitch of recognition.

He flicked on the light.

"Corey?" Logan asked, brows furrowing.

The young man blinked, his arms lifted halfway in surrender. "Logan?"

Corey was barely twenty-one, lean and jittery, his face familiar from the local grocery store—where he'd always gone out of his way to help Logan bag groceries or carry them to the car.

"You robbing me, Corey?" Logan asked, his tone casual, but edged with steel.

Corey glanced nervously at the shattered door, then around the room. "Hey, man... I didn't know you lived here."

Logan's expression remained unreadable. "No worries. You always take good care of me at the store."

"Just doing my job," Corey muttered.

Drawn by the view, Corey wandered toward the floor-to-ceiling windows. He paused, mouth open. "Wow."

"You do know I could've pulled the plug on you almost immediately," Logan said.

Corey turned back to face him, hands open. "Hey... I need the money. My mom's sick. No insurance."

Logan nodded. "Understood. But you walked in blind. Didn't know who you were targeting. That's a dangerous mistake, kid. Do your homework. Better yet—be smart. Stick to your day job. You'll live longer."

He reached into the pocket of his robe and pulled out a thick wad of cash. Without counting, he peeled off several large bills and held them out.

"This should help," Logan said. "Take care of your mom. And don't let me see you doing this again. Get the fuck out of here."

Corey's eyes widened. He stepped forward and took the money like it was holy. "Thanks, man. Really."

He bolted out the door, disappearing into the hallway like smoke.

Logan stood in silence, staring after him. The adrenaline still lingered in his veins, but his hands were steady. He glanced down at the fallen handgun, then back at the bed where Snoop now peeked from beneath the frame.

"Not your kind of excitement, huh?" he muttered.

The cat blinked at him.

Logan turned back to the view, still holding onto the weight of what hadn't happened.

The window framed the city like a living postcard—garish and shimmering in the late-morning sun. Vegas never slept, but even it had moments where the show dimmed just long enough to reveal the scaffolding underneath. He watched the cars drift down the boulevard like ants chasing sugar. From here, it all looked harmless. Clean, even.

He exhaled and pressed his hand against the glass. The cool surface steadied him. Outside, the illusion held. Inside, the room, sweat and fear lingered. Fear he would kill an innocent.

He'd seen it in Corey's face—that flicker of panic, the frozen moment when he became aware that he was in the presence of a man who'd already decided what he was capable of. The kid had been a split-second away from dying without knowing why.

But Logan had let him walk.

And that made him dangerous in a different way. It meant he still cared who lived.

He reached down and retrieved the fallen handgun, turning it once in his palm. The weight was familiar, but welcome. He placed it on the desk near the lamp, far from the reach of instinct.

Behind him, Snoop padded out from beneath the bed, tail flicking once in silent judgment. Logan watched the cat leap gracefully onto the windowsill and sit, content to track the city below like a predator with nowhere to be.

"You think I should've done it," Logan said, not as a question but a confession.

Snoop flicked one ear.

Logan ran a hand down his face, dragging fatigue with it. He hadn't slept in two days. Probably wouldn't sleep tonight either. Not with Parker circling. Not with money missing. Not with the kid now loose and talking, no matter how grateful, he might talk.

Still... he'd seen something in Corey. Or maybe in himself.

He wasn't sure which scared him more.

He walked over to the desk, pulled open the drawer, and found what he expected. Stationery. He grabbed the pen beside it and scrawled a name across the top.

Just a first name.

Just in case.

He tore the page off and tucked it into his coat.

Snoop meowed once, low, and impatient. "Yeah, I hear you," Logan muttered.

He stepped over to bar and picked up the bottle of Jura Scotch, hoping the alcohol would ease the thoughts in his mind. He came close to killing a kid. *A Kid.* He had to be more careful. Enough bad stuff resided in his mind, and orphaning and killing kids would be torturous even for a killer, at least this killer.

Outside, a siren wailed—closer this time.

Logan glanced toward the hallway. His fingers flexed once, then stilled.

# CHAPTER 15

The Venetian Hotel lobby shimmered beneath the brilliance of grand chandeliers, each crystal reflecting the morning light that spilled through tall arched windows. Marble floors stretched in all directions, polished to a glossy sheen that mirrored the opulence above. Ornate columns framed the room, with intricate gold leaf accents curling upward toward a painted ceiling of cherubs and cloud-scattered blue. The scent of fresh lilies wafted in from grand floral arrangements strategically placed across the room, and the gentle splash of water from a nearby indoor fountain added to the luxurious ambiance.

Brad Morgan and Dave Thompson entered the lobby, pulling wheeled suitcases behind them, their footsteps muffled by the plush oriental rugs that broke the expanse of marble. Brad's eyes darted around the space with unease, still on edge from the chaos back home. Dave, however, looked perfectly at ease—his gaze already locked on the woman behind the front desk.

The hotel clerk, a striking brunette with a nameplate that read *Melanie*, offered them a polite, professional smile.

"Good morning. Welcome to the Venetian."

Brad stepped forward, adjusting the strap of his duffel bag. "Good morning. I'm Mr. Morgan. I have a reservation for a double."

She tapped swiftly on the keyboard, her smile never faltering. "Yes, Mr. Morgan. We have reserved room sixteen eighty-eight. The bellhop will escort you to your room."

Before the bellhop could even approach, Dave leaned his elbows on the counter, eyes narrowing flirtatiously as he studied Melanie. "Would you like to come to our room after your shift?"

Brad shot him a look and elbowed him in the ribs—not hard, but enough to send a message.

Melanie blushed, glancing down at the monitor with an awkward smile as she avoided Dave's gaze.

Unbothered, Dave winked. "I'll check on you later, sweetheart."

With that, the two men followed the bellhop toward the elevators. The golden doors slid open, and as they stepped inside, the world of marble and wealth disappeared behind them, sealed off with a soft mechanical hum.

The hotel room was a testament to indulgence—lavish without being gaudy, its interior lined with rich, cream-colored walls and deep mahogany accents. A velvet settee rested near the foot of two plush queen beds, each topped with decorative pillows arranged with mathematical precision. The scent of citrus polish lingered in the air, evidence of recent cleaning. Golden sconces cast a warm glow against the high ceiling, while soft instrumental music played from hidden speakers, barely audible over the distant hum of Las Vegas life below.

The bellhop rolled in their luggage with practiced ease, the wheels whispering across the thick carpet. Brad handed him a folded bill, nodding in thanks. With a quick "Enjoy your stay," the bellhop disappeared into the hallway, letting the door click shut behind him.

Dave beelined for the floor-to-ceiling window, spreading the curtains wide. Morning sunlight poured in, illuminating the entire room in golden hues. He whistled low, pressing both palms to the glass as he took in the sprawling view of the Strip—casino towers, neon signs, and the endless dance of color and promise.

"This is unbelievable," Dave said, eyes glued to the scene outside. "Look at this view. My wife would kill for this view."

Brad smirked, unzipping his suitcase at the foot of the nearest bed. "Then maybe you should've invited her along."

Dave chuckled, still gazing out the window. "It would've been a short trip."

He turned away from the glass, rubbing his hands together with anticipation. "Let's hit the casino."

Brad shook his head as he pulled out a fresh shirt. "I want to shower and change first."

Dave gave a shrug and grabbed his wallet from the nightstand. "Well, my body odor is just fine. I'll see you downstairs."

Without waiting for a response, he slipped out the door. Alone now, Brad moved deliberately, neatly hanging his shirts in the closet, placing toiletries by the bathroom sink. He paused at the window, staring down at the streets below, but his gaze didn't linger. Instead, he turned toward the bathroom, shoulders heavy, mind already racing through numbers, odds, and silent, desperate prayers.

The gambling floor at the Venetian shimmered with artificial light and whispered with promise. Slot machines blinked in a kaleidoscope of colors, erupting into occasional jingles and fanfares. The constant clatter of chips on felt-covered tables filled the air, along with the clinking of glasses and the low murmur of dealers calling bets. The atmosphere throbbed with adrenaline, desperation, and desire—all camouflaged beneath designer suits and sequined dresses.

Brad slipped through the crowd and approached a blackjack table. His expression was unreadable—neither excitement nor dread on his face, only calculation. He slid into a seat and placed a modest bet to start. The cards came and went. A win. Then a loss. A few more wins. His eyes remained focused, though his jaw tightened each time the dealer's hand beat his.

Across the room, a striking blonde in a low-cut silk blouse took notice. Her gaze was cool and appraising. She had the poise of someone who was used to getting attention and the confidence to command it. After a moment, she sauntered over, heels clicking on the marble floor.

"I haven't seen you here before," she said, stopping beside him. Her voice purred, playful. "Is this your first time?"

Brad glanced sideways at her. His lips quirked, "Who wants to know?"

She extended her manicured hand. "Cindy. Cindy Reinholt."

Brad accepted it, his grip firm but brief. "Hello, Cindy. Are you the welcoming committee?"

There was a flicker of amusement in her eyes. "Maybe. I just find you... interesting. Your mannerisms. Your, well—how can I say it—your detachment."

"Detachment?" he repeated, turning back to the table.

"Yes. Like your body's here but your mind is somewhere far away." She tilted her head, studying him. "Are you hoping to win big?"

Brad laughed. "This is Vegas."

"It's rarely just about the gambling," she replied. "There's always something else—some secret, some unfinished business. Unless you're actually on vacation."

"Vacation? No. Sorry to disappoint. I need money, and lots of it." He gestured at the table. "Do you have any?"

He didn't even look at her when he said it. It was the kind of line that could've been rude, even insulting. But from Brad, it landed as flat honesty. Cindy raised her brows, intrigued.

"Are you asking me for money?" she asked.

"And that's all I'm asking for."

She should've walked away. Any reasonable woman would have. But Cindy didn't. There was something magnetic about his candor, his wounded pride barely hidden beneath a veil of sarcasm.

"Nothing else lights you up?" she asked.

Brad turned to face her, his eyes momentarily softening. "Only the torch my wife carries."

Cindy smirked. "So, she's a walking fire hazard?"

"An amazing fire hazard," Brad replied. "You won't know you got burned until months later." He chuckled under his breath. "And even then... you still feel good."

He turned his attention back to the table and said, "Hit me." Even though he held a solid seventeen.

The dealer flipped the card. "A five, that's twenty-two."

Brad sighed. "At this rate, I'm in trouble."

Cindy leaned in and whispered something close to his ear. He raised his eyebrows, amused. "Okay, I'll try that." He tapped the table, signaling the dealer to pass out the next two cards. Brad sat on sixteen and won because the dealer busted.

Brad grinned. "Now we're talking. What else you got?"

Cindy whispered again.

Brad tapped again. The dealer dealt, and every Blackjack player's dream came true for him. Ace and King of Spades. A thing of beauty.

"Yes!" Brad's grin widened. "You are my lucky charm."

She stayed by his side as he placed more bets, each one guided by her subtle suggestions. Steadily, his stack of chips grew.

Then a familiar voice rang out behind him.

"Hey man, I've already won five grand and it's barely lunchtime!"

Dave clapped a hand on Brad's shoulder, grinning from ear to ear. His eyes shifted to Cindy. "I see you've met."

Brad glanced between the two of them, suspicious. "You know each other?"

Cindy gave Brad a nod, her lips curving into a sly smile.

"Brad, this is the friend I was telling you about," Dave said, planting a kiss on Cindy's cheek. "Tell her the story. She might be able to help."

Cindy turned to Brad with new clarity in her eyes. "Oh... you're the one in trouble."

"That would be me," Brad said, his voice dry. "And I don't have much time."

"I'll catch up with you guys later," Dave said, already eyeing a tall redhead walking past.

"Oh—there's a message from your wife at the front desk," Brad said.

Dave shoots him a snide look. "Ok, green doesn't look good on you."

"I'm not jealous, not even a little bit." Brad snorted, then watched as Dave wandered off, his gaze hopping from one woman to the next.

Cindy turned back toward Brad. "I heard you have a serious problem."

"Unless you have a lot of money," he said, "you can't help me."

She didn't flinch. "I can help."

Brad looked at her, genuinely curious now. "Let's go somewhere private. I'll tell you my tale... Tell you my tale. Not bad, right?"

Cindy laughed. "Yeah, really funny." She leaned in. "Let's go. I know just the place."

Brad grabbed his chips, slid them into his pocket, and followed her through the casino crowd, the lights flashing overhead like stars made of neon and broken dreams.

# CHAPTER 16

The valet pulled the sleek silver Porsche Panamera around the curved entrance of the casino, its engine humming with quiet power. The car's body caught the gleaming desert sun, reflecting sharp glints as heads turned to admire the luxury vehicle.

Brad whistled under his breath. "Nice."

Cindy smiled and handed the valet a crisp bill before sliding effortlessly behind the wheel. Brad circled around and got in on the passenger side, shutting the door just as the car shot forward with a smooth surge of acceleration.

Inside, the scent of leather and high-end perfume mingled with the purr of the engine. Brad reached for his seat belt, snapping it into place as Cindy veered confidently into traffic on the busy Las Vegas strip.

She drove fast—too fast—navigating the congested lanes with practiced ease, weaving through cars like a pro on a racetrack. Brad tightened his grip on the door handle, his stomach dropping as they narrowly missed a lumbering Mack truck changing lanes without warning.

"So, you're a gambler too," Brad said, trying to sound casual despite his quickened pulse.

Cindy glanced over, amused. "What?"

"It's pretty obvious. You like to take risks."

She laughed, a low, unbothered sound. "No one's after me, if that's what you're thinking."

The car swerved to the right, narrowly avoiding a cab that braked too late.

Brad pressed back into the seat. "I was hoping that wasn't the case."

"No, silly," she said, cutting across two lanes without signaling. "I just love to drive fast. It gets my heart pumping."

Brad chuckled, though he was still gripping the edge of his seat. "Yeah, mine too. Feels like it's about to explode."

"Relax," she said, eyes on the road but voice steady. "Trust me—I have too much to live for."

Brad turned and studied her for a moment. The way her jaw was set, the way her eyes flicked between mirrors and lanes with instinctual control—it was clear she wasn't reckless. She was deliberate. Dangerous, but in full command.

He exhaled and leaned back, watching the city blur past them in streaks of neon and sunlight, wondering if he'd just stepped into something far more complicated than he'd expected.

⋯⋯◆⋯⋯

The Porsche screeched into the driveway of the Spartus Club, its sleek black frame catching the shimmer of neon lights under the Vegas sky. Cindy gripped the wheel with confidence, spinning it with a casual flick before bringing the car to a halt. She stepped out in one fluid motion, tossing the keys to the valet with a smirk and a wink. Brad emerged from the passenger side a little slower, straightening the front of his shirt as his eyes took in the opulence around him.

"Nice," he muttered, trailing behind Cindy toward the club's glowing entrance.

Inside, the Spartus Club pulsed with life. The air shimmered with heat and sound—bass-heavy music thumped against the walls like a second heartbeat. A sea of bodies in their twenties and thirties moved to the music under a canopy of crystal lights. The scent of perfume and liquor filled the air.

Brad and Cindy pushed their way through the crowd until they found a narrow opening at the bar. Cindy leaned against the counter, her posture as confident as her heels were high.

"You know," Brad said, raising his voice over the music, "we could've had a drink at the hotel. Why here? This is not exactly... quiet."

She flashed him a knowing look, her eyes glinting beneath heavy lashes. "You're going to be at that hotel all week," she said. "This—this is a little diversity. A slight change of scene. Relax."

Brad exhaled and turned his gaze toward the crowd. "You know, it's a little irritating being told to relax all the time."

"Okay then," she said with a laugh, "Loosen up. You're so up-tight."

A bartender—a man who could've stepped off a billboard—appeared in front of them. He was tall, bronze-skinned, with perfectly sculpted arms and a smolder that could melt glass.

"What can I get you?" he asked.

Cindy didn't hesitate. "I'll have a dirty martini. Extremely dirty. Filthy." Her eyes danced up and down the bartender as if she were undressing him with each syllable. He smirked in response, enjoying the attention.

Brad shifted on his stool, annoyed. "I'll have a scotch," he said, terse.

The bartender turned to him with a courteous nod. "Absolutely, sir. I'll be right back with your orders." He cast one final glance at Cindy before disappearing down the bar.

Cindy turned back to Brad, eyes gleaming. "Let's dance," she said.

Brad raised an eyebrow. "I can't dance. I sway."

"Fine," she grinned, grabbing his hand. "Let's sway."

She dragged him onto the dance floor, pressing close as the music shifted into a slow, seductive rhythm. Her hips rolled like waves in a storm. Brad did his best to follow, his movements were less fluid but earnest.

"You have some sexy moves," Cindy said, her lips brushing his ear. "If you weren't married, I'd have my way with you... over and over again... you'd forget your wife's name."

Brad's smile faltered. He glanced down at his left hand, his wedding band catching the glow of strobe lights. "Let's leave my wife out of this."

Cindy inched closer. "I don't have a problem with that."

The music ended, but for Brad, it didn't end soon enough. He was beginning to enjoy the closeness, which would not be good. They returned to the bar just as the drinks arrived. Cindy sipped hers with satisfaction.

"There's a way to make a lot of money," she said, leaning in. "If you're not afraid of taking risks. Real risks."

She pulled a cigarette from her purse and lit it with a practiced flair, exhaling a curl of smoke toward the ceiling. Her gaze locked on Brad.

"I wonder if I can trust you," she added.

Brad gave a faint chuckle, one corner of his mouth lifting. "That depends. What exactly are we talking about here?"

"My life," she said. "Basically, we're talking about my life here. Can I trust you with it?"

Brad's tone softened. "You can trust that I won't take it."

"Seriously," she said, her voice lower. "Do you have a business card? A driver's license? I have to be careful."

Brad retrieved his wallet from his back pocket and tossed it onto the bar. Cindy caught it mid-air and flipped it open with nimble fingers. Her eyes scanned over his employee ID.

"Oh, you sell life insurance? Like Dave? Do you two work together?"

"Almost daily," Brad replied, sipping his scotch.

"Life insurance. That has to be awfully boring."

"It pays the bills... when I'm not gambling."

"You live in Joliet, Illinois?"

Brad nodded. "Yeah. And?"

"Small town."

"That's why I like it."

Cindy kept flipping. She paused at a business card.

Morgan's Karate School      Brad Morgan      Instructor
555-555-5555

"You teach karate?" she asked, raising an eyebrow.

Brad mimicked a slow martial arts stance with exaggerated grace. "Would you like to learn some moves?"

She laughed, handing the wallet back. "No thanks."

She studied him, a little more seriously now. "I think you're safe. You won't take me home and have me for dinner."

"If I don't eat soon," he said, "I *will* have you for dinner. Do they serve food here?"

"Absolutely," she said, motioning for a waiter. "Let's get a table."

The waiter guided them to a small candlelit booth in the corner, handing them menus with a polite nod.

"Should I come back?" the waiter asked.

Brad shook his head. "No, I think we're ready. Cindy?"

"I'll have the Swissvale linguini with broccoli," she said, handing over the menu. "And another Dirty Apple Martini."

"Of course, madam," the waiter replied with a courteous bow.

"T-bone special," Brad added. "Baked potato. French dressing for the salad. And another scotch."

The waiter gave a small bow. "Certainly."

As he walked off, Cindy leaned forward.

"You must be nervous," she said.

Brad didn't hesitate. "I am nervous. You're so damn beautiful."

"There are beautiful women everywhere."

"True," he said, his voice dropping. "But there's only one sitting a few inches from me right now. Looking at me with those big blue eyes. A bad girl who likes to take risks... You have no idea how attractive that is to me. Hey... I'm lit."

Cindy arched an eyebrow. "What will your wife say?"

Brad smiled. "Who?"

They laughed together.

The waiter returned with their drinks. Brad raised his glass and took a sip.

"Seriously," he said. "I love my wife. But you... you are definitely a test of my willpower."

"There's nothing wrong with a little flirtation, is there?" Cindy asked.

Brad raised his glass in a small toast. "I guess time will tell."

The waiter returned again, this time carrying their plates. Brad's eyes lit up.

"Oh, this looks good."

# CHAPTER 17

Cindy's Porsche coasted into the long driveway of her elegant country home, the tires crunching over loose gravel. The house stood majestically beneath the night sky, its modern architecture softened by warm porch lights and the rustling of wind in tall pines. She cut the engine, and both she and Brad stepped out into the cool air. Together, they walked up the path to the front door. Cindy produced a key, unlocked it, and ushered him inside.

"Wow," Brad said as he stepped through the threshold, his eyes scanning the spacious interior. "This is nice."

Cindy gave a slight smile. "Thanks. It's my castle."

"You live here alone?"

"Yes. I have a daughter, Cassie... she lives in Newark now." She gestured toward the sunken living room. "Have a seat. I'll get you a drink."

Brad stepped down into the cozy space and wandered toward a wall lined with framed photographs. One showed a young girl—Cassie, he assumed—and beside her, a man with a tight-lipped smile and eyes that hinted at unfinished stories. Likely the ex-husband.

Behind him, Cindy called out, "At the bar I noticed you like Scotch."

"I do like Scotch," Brad answered, turning toward her. "What do you do, Cindy, to afford a place like this?"

"I could tell you," she said, carrying over two glasses, "but then I'd have to kill you."

Brad laughed. "Ha. Ha."

"I've always wanted to say that. Makes me feel like Jennifer Bond."

She handed him a glass and took a sip from her own.

Brad looked at her over the rim of his drink. "Is the question too personal?"

Cindy hesitated only a moment. "No, it's not. I... I steal. I'm good at stealing. It's how I make my living." She studied his reaction. "Are you shocked?"

Brad blinked. "It wouldn't have been my first guess. A beautiful woman like you—"

Her expression hardened. "You think I slept my way to the top? That all beautiful women must be using their bodies?"

Brad raised his hands. "Wouldn't you agree that in the majority of cases, that's what beautiful women do? Find a rich schmuck and milk him dry?"

Cindy's voice sharpened. "That's so stereotypical. I hate that. We're not all whores."

"I'm sorry," Brad said, genuinely. "I didn't mean to offend."

She sighed and moved toward the sofa, her tone softening again. "Look, I could use someone on my side. I got greedy last week and crossed into territory I probably shouldn't have."

"You want to start from the beginning?"

Cindy walked to a shelf near the stereo. She pulled out a classic Sinatra record, lifted the needle, and set it on the phonograph. Soft music from another era drifted into the room, smooth and steady.

She nodded. "I stole money from the casino... a lot of money."

Brad let the words settle in the air.

"Usually," Cindy continued, "I worked the tables, and I knew how to pull in some good money. But... I got greedy."

Brad turned to her. "Did you pull this off by yourself?"

"Yes, I thought about asking my friend Logan to help, but I didn't want to be responsible for the risk he would also be taking, just for me."

"Wouldn't this Logan guy know you stole the money?"

She shook her head. "He would never suspect me. He doesn't know what I do. He thinks I'm innocent and needs protecting."

"Innocent?" Brad asked.

"Yes. And I was, for many years." Her voice became distant. "Until I decided I wanted money to buy whatever I wanted—whether I was with a man or not. I wanted to depend on me."

She paused, her fingers tightening around the base of her glass.

"When I wanted a lover, it was my choice. Not theirs. And it didn't depend on how much money they had. I had my own. I liked that."

Brad moved to her side, crouched, and took her hands in his. "So, what's the problem now?"

"I've been getting strange calls in the middle of the night," she said. "Someone just breathes into the phone, then hangs up. And sometimes... I feel like someone's watching me. Maybe it's just in my head. But it's freaking me out."

"It's just nerves," Brad said. "How much did you take?"

She met his eyes. "Three million."

Brad blinked, pulling the words apart like pieces of a bomb. "Three *mil-lion* dollars?"

She nodded without flinching.

Cindy walked over to the sofa and sat down. Brad followed and settled in beside her.

"Where's the money now?"

"In the tree house," she replied. "I've been laundering it. I don't know if it's marked."

"If it's casino money, it's not marked. But that's a lot of money."

"If you and Dave can help me safely leave town, I'll pay you a million dollars. Gladly."

Brad let out a breath. "So, you're recruiting me to be your guardian angel?"

She took another sip from her glass, her hesitation returning.

"Dave said you needed money and could help. But if you aren't interested—"

"I'm definitely interested," Brad interrupted. "But I don't have a lot of time. Only about forty-eight hours now..."

He paused, studying her. "Where do you plan to go?"

"Back to Newark. My daughter's father is there. It's as good a place as any. I'll have enough money to live comfortably and do something more legit."

Brad leaned back, processing it all. "We need to move fast."

"Tomorrow?" she asked.

"Early a.m."

She nodded and rose from the couch. "You can sleep in my daughter's room tonight. Come with me."

———◦———

The bedroom was a sharp departure from the elegance of the rest of the house. The walls, painted a moody charcoal gray, were plastered with Marilyn Manson posters—one of them peeling in the corner. An old lava lamp flickered on the nightstand, casting sluggish, red-orange blobs against the dark surfaces. A human skull replica sat atop the dresser, its hollow sockets facing the bed like a silent sentinel. The space pulsed with teen rebellion and angst, a sharp contrast to Cindy's composed and sensual demeanor.

Brad sat on the edge of the bed, his eyes taking in the room's gothic details.

"Looks like your daughter has an identification problem," he muttered, half to himself.

Cindy leaned against the doorframe, arms crossed, her face touched with both amusement and sadness. "She's finding her way."

Just then, Brad's phone buzzed in his pocket. He pulled it out. The screen lit up with a familiar name: *Mary*.

Cindy caught the name and backed out, leaving the door partially ajar. Brad took a breath and answered.

"Hello, sweetheart."

Mary's voice was soft, strained from fatigue. "Hey... what's going on? We haven't talked."

"Just getting settled," Brad replied, glancing at the posters again. "What did the doctor say?"

"Everything checked out. I could go into labor any day now." Mary continued. "Brad, I need you to be here."

Brad lowered his head. The guilt crept in through his chest and settled in his throat like acid. "I know. I'll do my best. But we need money, that's why I'm here."

"You're staying on budget, right?"

He rubbed his temple, thinking about Cindy, the million-dollar offer, the dance, the drinks, the three million in a treehouse. "I'm watching the money. Don't worry."

"Maybe next year we can do it together."

Brad forced a smile, one she couldn't see. "No way. Hawaii. Vegas can wait."

"Wherever you want to go. You decide."

"Look sweetheart, I'll call you tomorrow. Love you. Bye."

"Love you too. Bye."

He ended the call and stared at the phone. For a moment, everything was still. Then the door creaked open again.

Cindy stepped inside wearing a skimpy negligee, soft silk that shimmered in the hallway light behind her. Her blonde hair fell over one shoulder, and her hips moved with practiced ease as she walked to the dresser to tidy a few things.

Brad blinked. "Mrs. Robinson, you're trying to seduce me."

Cindy paused. "What?"

He smirked. "Never mind. Just a line in a movie."

She looked over her shoulder. "Oh yeah, *The Graduate*."

"You saw the movie?"

"Hasn't everyone?"

Brad shrugged. "No, not everyone."

She gave a wry smile, adjusted a framed picture of Cassie that had tilted on the shelf, then turned and walked out of the room without another word.

Brad sat there a moment longer, running his hands through his hair. Then he stood, grabbed a clean towel from the chair, and headed to the bathroom for a long, much-needed shower. The distant echo of Sinatra's voice still floated through the house, romantic and dangerous all at once.

# CHAPTER 18

The smell of sizzling eggs drifted through the air, mingling with the faint echo of last night's conversation. Sunlight poured in through half-open blinds, dusting the countertops in gold.

Cindy stood barefoot at the stove, her silk robe hanging loosely around her shoulders. She flipped the eggs with sharp, practiced motions, the skillet popping beneath her. The air was warm with heat and tension.

Brad stepped into the kitchen, his hair damp from the shower, his shirt wrinkled and half-buttoned. He looked like a man suspended—neither fully dressed nor completely undone. He sank into a chair at the small wooden table.

She didn't turn to greet him. "Do you know how to shoot?"

He frowned. "A gun?"

"No, a camera." She spun with the spatula in her hand, sarcasm biting at the edge of her voice. "Yes, a gun."

Brad shrugged. "I can aim. I can pull the trigger."

Cindy stared at him—hard. Her eyes, once flirtatious and teasing, now held a different fire. Disappointment. Maybe even fear.

Without another word, she returned to the stove, scraped the eggs onto a plate, and walked it over. She heaped a mountain of eggs onto Brad's plate and less onto her own. Then, she opened the refrigerator, pulled out a carton of orange juice, and poured two glasses. The tension between them clung like smoke.

They sat at the table. No music. No laughter. Just the scrape of silverware and the occasional hiss of the cooling skillet.

Cindy didn't look up. "This was a mistake."

Brad blinked. "Excuse me?"

"You're too green. You'll get us both killed."

He lowered his fork. "Wow. Okay."

"You should go back home," she said. "You can't help me."

"I didn't come here to help you," Brad snapped, the calm in his voice now threadbare. "I came to Vegas to gamble. To win big."

Cindy leaned back, arms folded. "I don't see any big wins. You made a few pennies. That's nothing. Tomorrow you'll be broke again."

Brad scoffed, eyes narrowing. "You think I'm a loser?"

Her fork clattered onto the plate as she stood up. Her voice was cold steel.

"Well, aren't you?"

That did it.

Brad rose from the table. His breathing had changed—deeper now, heavier. He looked at her for a long second, then grabbed his plate and, without warning, hurled it at the wall. It shattered with a thunderous crash, yellow scrambled eggs splattering against white plaster.

He didn't say another word. He turned and stormed out of the kitchen.

Brad marched down the quiet, tree-lined street, his hands shoved in his pockets, his jaw clenched. The air was crisp, the kind of chill that bites right through your shirt. Each step was sharp, angry.

But the words followed him, louder than his footsteps.

*"Well, aren't you?"*

He gritted his teeth.

*"Well, aren't you?"*

He walked faster.

———◄O►———

Cindy stood frozen in the kitchen, staring at the broken plate, at the mess on her wall. Her chest rose and fell in quick bursts. She wasn't sure if she was angry or afraid or something else altogether.

With shaking hands, she grabbed her keys from the counter and headed toward the door.

She wasn't ready to let him walk away. Not yet.

———◄O►———

The sun was already warming the pavement as Cindy threw open the door of her sleek silver Porsche, slid into the driver's seat, and slammed it shut with purpose. Without hesitation, she backed down the drive and sped through the neighborhood, her jaw set tight. A few blocks away, she spotted Brad walking with his head down, kicking gravel as he went. She slowed beside him and rolled the window down.

"Get in," she snapped.

Brad didn't stop. "Do you make a habit of picking up losers?"

"I won't apologize!" she barked, leaning across the passenger seat. "Get in!"

He halted, glanced at her through narrowed eyes. "What do you want from me?"

"I have a plan," she said, her tone lower now, tighter. "Get the fuck in the car."

Something in her voice pulled at him—ferocity, certainty, maybe desperation. Whatever it was, he liked it. He opened the door and slid in, keeping his gaze on her. There was something magnetic about the sharpness in her edges. Something he didn't know how to fight.

They drove in silence, Cindy's hands firm on the wheel. She didn't look at him, didn't explain. The Porsche sliced through the outskirts of Vegas and veered off the main road, winding toward a more isolated area where the city's glitter faded behind them.

Eventually, the car pulled into the gravel drive of a small farm. The buildings were weathered and sun-bleached. Cindy parked near a rundown barn and turned off the engine.

"Wait here."

She climbed out without waiting for a response and disappeared inside the barn. A few minutes later, she returned with two hand-guns. She motioned for Brad to get out.

He stepped out, eyeing the weapons. "What is this about?"

"Aiming and pulling the trigger," she said with a smirk.

Then she turned and started walking toward a narrow path leading into a back field. Brad followed, still not sure if this was insane or brilliant. A part of him didn't care.

They emerged into a clearing marked with old crates and tin cans balanced on fenceposts. Rusted targets dotted the field, riddled with bullet holes from past practice. Cindy handed him one of the handguns and took her position beside him.

"I need you to be able to handle a gun," she said.

"You could hire someone for that."

"I could," she said, lifting the other weapon. "But could I trust them?"

He looked at her, trying to decipher whether it was a compliment or a test. "So, you trust me?"

"I do."

What followed was quiet instruction layered with patience and grit. Cindy moved with fluid control, guiding his stance, correcting his grip, repositioning his shoulders. Brad tried, missed the target by a foot. She didn't flinch.

Again.

Another miss—six inches off.

She adjusted him. Coached him.

A third shot—three inches off.

Her eyes didn't waver.

Again.

The gun cracked. The bullet struck dead center.

Bullseye.

Cindy gave a half-smile, half-smirk, and said, "Good. Now let's see if you can do it twice."

# CHAPTER 19

The night was thick with tension as Cindy steered the Porsche back into her driveway. The gravel crunched beneath the tires, headlights sweeping across the front porch like a searchlight through darkness. The engine went quiet, but the pulse of danger still echoed between them. Brad stepped out, glancing at the sky as if expecting it to fall.

They entered through the back door, the kitchen bathed in soft amber light. It should have felt safe—familiar even—but Cindy moved like a shadow, her shoulders rigid with worry.

"We need to leave as soon as possible," she said, tossing her keys on the counter with a clatter. "I just don't feel comfortable anymore."

Brad nodded, brushing the hair off his brow. "I have to go to the hotel first, talk to Dave, grab my clothes. We could stop there on the way out of town."

"You can back out if you want," she said, almost like a dare. "I'll understand."

Brad turned toward her, eyes hollow yet burning. "I have a bomb ticking inside of me. I need to take care of business and save my life right now."

Cindy froze mid-step. "You want to repeat that?"

"I owe a loan shark," he said, his voice low, a confession wrapped in steel. "He implanted a tracking device inside of me. He can detonate it whenever he wants. I don't have much time."

"Oh my God," she whispered, her hand lifting to her mouth.

"So you see, I'm desperate."

She looked him over like she was seeing him for the first time—gauging the man beneath the desperation.

"Are you in any pain?"

"Amazingly, no. But I know it's there."

She nodded, turning away to gather herself. "Let's get going. Can you get me a couple of boxes from the shed? There's some stuff in my daughter's room I need to take."

Brad stood, stepped toward her, and touched her arm. "Look, it's going to work out."

"I know," she said.

"I'm not a loser. I won't fail. My wife depends on me. She needs me."

With that, he stepped outside into the darkness. The air was thick, the kind that carries secrets.

The shed stood like an old sentinel near the edge of the property. Brad walked briskly, opened the creaking door, and stepped inside. Rows of rusting tools and lawn equipment lined the walls, a pile of broken-down cardboard boxes slumped in the corner like tired soldiers. He gathered what he could, arms full, ready to return—until something caught his eye.

Through the dusty windowpane, a sleek black car rolled to a stop in front of the house. Two men emerged, both armed, both moving with quiet, deadly purpose.

Brad's breath caught.

He set the boxes down and scanned the shed for anything he could use. No guns. Just junk. Until his eyes fell on the ax—old, but heavy. He grabbed it, gave it a few test swings in the air, then ducked out of the shed and into the shadows.

At the house, the men were already inside.

He crept to a rear window and peeked in. Cindy was backed into the kitchen, her eyes blazing with fear.

"Where's our money, Cindy?" one of them demanded.

"I don't know what you're talking about," she said, her voice steely.

The first man circled her, then struck her—hard. She hit the floor.

"You have about one minute," said the second. "Then we stop asking questions."

"I don't have the money!" she shouted.

The first one yanked her to her feet by the hair. "We'll kill you. Understand?"

She nodded, lips trembling. "It's in the tree house."

"Lead the way," the second said.

Brad didn't wait. He darted through the bushes, heart hammering, eyes tracking every step they took toward the wooden steps of the tree house.

From behind cover, Brad watched them go inside.

"Where is the money?" the second man asked.

Cindy moved with shaky confidence. She went behind a bookcase, pulled out the briefcase, and handed it over. He flipped it open, started counting.

In the shadows, Brad crouched closer, creeping toward the staircase.

"Is it all there?" the first man asked.

"Every green bill," said the second.

"What do we do with this one?" he asked, glancing at Cindy. "We don't need her anymore."

"We've been instructed to let her be."

"I've never followed instructions."

He raised his gun to Cindy's temple.

A loud CRACK echoed from below.

Both men spun, one threw open the treehouse door. Nothing.

Brad darted to the side, crouching low, the ax poised in his hands. As they shoved Cindy down the steps, he sprang.

The blade landed with a sickening crunch into the second man's back. He dropped instantly, dead before he hit the grass.

Brad twisted toward the first shooter, delivered a hard, precise karate chop to his wrist. The gun clattered to the dirt. Brad pressed the ax to the man's throat.

"Don't move."

Cindy scrambled to pick up the fallen gun.

"I need something to tie him with," Brad said.

"I've got rope at the house. Let's go."

She grabbed the briefcase. Brad jabbed the axe at the man's back, forcing him to his feet. The three of them marched in grim silence to the house.

Inside, Brad shoved the man into a chair. Cindy retrieved the rope, her hands shaking as she passed it over. Brad tied the man tight.

"You're making a mistake," the man growled. "There are others. They'll come."

"Probably," Brad said.

"They'll kill you. Her too."

Brad leaned close. "You need to shut the hell up."

Cindy hovered nearby, her face pale. Brad turned to her.

"Duct tape?"

"Uh, maybe. Maybe in the shed."

"Can you check?"

She nodded and fled outside. Brad stood alone with the tied man.

"You're smart," the shooter said. "Get out now. Let her go. She's poison."

Brad glared.

"She'll drag you into a grave."

That did it. Brad surged forward, grabbing the chair and shaking it violently.

"Shut the fuck up!"

The man did.

Brad slumped in the kitchen chair, elbows on knees, head bowed. The ax still red with blood. He was breathing like a man who had run for miles.

Minutes passed.

Cindy returned with the tape. "Here," she said, holding it out. "Let's go."

"What about your daughter's things?"

"I can't think about that now. We need to leave."

Brad nodded, taping the man's mouth shut. He checked the knots, double-checked.

And then he saw it. The face. Unmistakable. One of the hooded bastards was one of the men who had stormed his house—who had put his pregnant wife in danger. Something cold and ancient flooded Brad's veins.

He stalked to the counter, picked up the largest kitchen knife he could find.

"Indeed, they lied," he muttered, half to himself. "This will hurt you more than it hurts me. Believe it."

Before Cindy could stop him, he drove the blade deep into the man's neck. Blood sprayed, painting the kitchen in crimson horror. The man convulsed, then went still.

Cindy gasped, hands over her mouth. Brad stared at his blood-soaked hands, the knife clattering to the floor like guilt itself.

"Let's go."

He grabbed the ax and the gun, following Cindy to the car. She popped the trunk. The briefcase went in. Brad returned the ax to the shed with haunted calm, then got in.

The engine roared to life. They left the house behind.

And behind it, a corpse bled out in the chair, silence finding a place to rest.

# CHAPTER 20

The smell of cigar smoke lingered thick in the air like a storm cloud refusing to pass. Parker leaned back in his leather chair, the weight of the day pressing into his spine. The administration room was quiet but for the soft whir of surveillance tapes looping on the monitors in front of him. Onscreen, the casino bustled with life—drinks clinked, chips clattered, and people lost their money with desperate smiles. He took another puff of his cigar, exhaled and squinted at the footage.

The phone on his desk rang, shrill and insistent.

He picked it up with two fingers. "Yeah."

The voice on the other end was grim, flat. "It didn't go well. Both Deck and Johnny are dead. Cindy had help. They got away. I'm sure she still has the money."

Parker didn't respond. He hung up, lips tightening around the cigar. The smoke curled around his head like a noose.

He turned back to the monitor and hit rewind. The image flickered, reversed, then stabilized on a scene from the previous day. He leaned forward. There she was—Cindy—laughing, charming, playing her part as always. But it wasn't her that held his attention now.

He pressed a button, zooming in.

Next to her, a man. Late thirties. Serious eyes. Nervous posture. Parker squinted and leaned closer to the screen. The man fumbled with a wallet—Brad.

"So, this is the bozo that helped you," Parker muttered.

He skipped through the footage, toggling through angles until another scene appeared—Cindy, Brad, and Dave together.

It was grainy, but clear enough. Cindy leaned in close to Brad at the Blackjack table, her hand on his wrist, her mouth just a breath from his ear. Dave was there too, distracted, laughing at something the dealer said, completely oblivious.

The pieces slid into place like a loaded chamber.

Parker leaned back in his chair, eyes narrowing. His jaw moved side to side, slow and tight, like a man grinding his teeth over a memory he couldn't quite crush.

So this is how it started.

He paused the frame. Cindy's face looked different here—brighter, younger, even a little reckless. But he knew better. He'd trained her to get close, trained her to find cracks in men and split them open with a whisper. And now she was using those skills with Brad Morgan.

Of all people.

Parker's hand hovered over the keyboard, fingers twitching with restrained fury. He clicked the mouse again, jumping back in time, scanning for the moment they entered the casino. More footage. More angles.

Elevator. Lobby. Bar. Room.

He watched her kiss Brad in the hallway like it was the easiest thing in the world. No hesitation. No shame.

Parker reached for the phone again, no hesitation in his fingers this time. He dialed a number with practiced ease, the kind you don't forget even after a decade of silence.

After a moment, a gruff voice answered, "Hello?"

Parker didn't bother with pleasantries.

"Come to my office. Right now."

He dropped the receiver back into its cradle, the click echoing through the massive, cold room.

Logan would be here shortly.

And when he arrived, the hunt would begin.

Parker stood, stretching his back. His reflection stared at him from the glass window overlooking the Vegas skyline—sharp suit, expensive tie, eyes like broken glass. He stepped closer to the window and watched the Strip breathe below him, all neon and decay.

He'd built his kingdom one debt at a time. One corpse at a time. And now it threatened to fall apart because of a woman he once trusted and a gambler too stupid to know he was being used.

Brad Morgan.

The name soured in his mouth. He should've cut that thread the second Morgan's father went rogue. But Parker had waited, watched. Leverage and timing— would decide.

Now the clock was ticking faster than he liked.

He turned back to the monitor. Replayed the hallway kiss. Froze it.

He could practically hear Cindy's voice in his head—soft, sultry, lying.

Parker opened a drawer in the desk and pulled out a file. Inside were surveillance photos, financial records, and copies of Brad's withdrawal slips. Sloppy. Obvious. A man unraveling.

And now, with his fingerprints all over Cindy?

That made him vulnerable.

Parker lit a cigarette and took a long drag, holding the smoke in his lungs as if it would slow his thoughts. He leaned against the edge of the desk, exhaled, and stared at the door.

Logan wouldn't knock. He never did.

And when he came in, there'd be no need for explanations. Just names. Just blood.

Parker flicked ash into a crystal tray and whispered to the empty room:

"Let's see how far they're willing to run."

# CHAPTER 21

The hotel room was dim, its curtains drawn except for a small gap where the city lights peeked through. Brad sat at the small table, hunched over a laptop, eyes locked on the monitor as he scrolled through files and flight information. Dave sat across from him, sipping from a glass of scotch, his usual wisecracks silenced by tension. Cindy stood near the window, gazing out at the glittering Vegas skyline, lost in thought.

"Cindy," Brad snapped, without looking up. "Close the curtains. Someone could be watching."

She turned, eyes flicking toward him, then pulled the heavy drapes shut. The room felt even smaller now, the outside world shut away.

Dave sighed and shook his head. "How are you going to fight them, Brad? You don't know shit about gangsters."

Brad didn't flinch. "I know I've got a wife who depends on me. That's all I need to know."

Dave snorted, raising his glass again. "Don't forget the child."

"I can't forget," Brad said.

Cindy crossed the room and placed a hand on Brad's shoulder. Her touch was soft but electric, her voice low. "At least you understand what kind of financial commitment fatherhood is. You're already ahead of most men."

Dave rolled his eyes. "Would you cut it out already? We've got work to do."

Cindy flashed him a grin. "Who's green now?"

Brad held up a hand. "Hey. We need to focus."

Dave leaned forward. "It's simple. We get in the car, drive to the airport, Cindy gets on a plane to Newark, and we go home. Done."

Brad shook his head. "It's not that simple if someone follows us. You know there's more at stake than just money."

Cindy nodded, her expression softening. "Yes. Family."

Dave drained the rest of his scotch and set the glass down with a clink. "My wife doesn't get to cash me out like this. She wants to leave me? Fine. But I'm not making it easy for her."

Brad returned to the laptop and tapped a few keys. "I'm booking you on a Newark flight that leaves in two hours," he said to Cindy. "Ours leaves around the same time."

Cindy leaned over his shoulder to look at the screen, her hair brushing against his cheek. Brad ignored the sensation, focusing on the itinerary. Meanwhile, Dave poured himself another drink.

Brad noticed. "Dave... stay in Vegas. Gamble. Be safe. There's no need for you to risk your life. Like you said—we don't know how to fight gangsters."

Dave slammed the glass down harder than necessary. "I'm not running out on you. We're in this together. I want to help."

Cindy tilted her head, smirking. "Now who's coming on to who? This is starting to sound like a love story."

Brad stood, grinning. Dave followed. They wrapped each other in an exaggerated hug and pretended to sob.

"I'm with you, man," Dave said, voice quivering with theatrical drama. "All the way."

"Have I told you lately," Brad replied, matching his tone, "how much your support means to me?"

Cindy shook her head, chuckling. For a moment, the tension in the room lifted.

---

Across town, the mood was darker.

Parker sat alone in the administration office, a haze of cigar smoke circling his head like a crown of ash. He reclined in his chair, facing the large window that overlooked a quiet alley behind the casino. The phone call had already been made.

Logan stepped through the door, tall, composed, and unreadable.

Parker turned around to face him, the cigar clenched between his teeth. "Logan, I wanted to thank you personally for the McPherson job last week. It could've blown up in our faces. You were discreet. Professional."

"I was just doing my job," Logan replied. "But I know that's not why you called me here. What's going on?"

"That bitch Carol, stole from me," Parker growled. "And I think she had help."

Logan's voice didn't waver. "You want the money returned?"

"I want her dead," Parker said flatly. "And her accomplices. I don't like betrayal."

Logan took a moment. "Does she have kids?"

Parker narrowed his eyes. "What the hell is it with you? I don't know if she's got rug rats. It never got that deep. Are you taking the job or do I need someone with fewer questions?"

"I'll do it," Logan said. "What do you know?"

Parker jabbed a finger at the monitors. "Review the tapes. That's what I pay you for—do your job."

Logan nodded and turned to go. As he stepped through the door, Parker leaned back again, cigar back in his mouth, his gaze drifting to the window.

The hunt had begun.

# CHAPTER 22

Logan sat in the clean, modern lines of his home office, bathed in the cool glow of the monitor. A glass of Jura Scotch rested within reach, the ice melting untouched for several minutes. The city lights outside painted soft reflections on the black lacquer of his desk. Everything around him was order, precision—sterile, just the way he liked it.

He clicked through the surveillance footage with the same calm deliberation he gave to everything—no emotion, no wasted movement. The casino's grainy security reels flickered across the screen. One by one, he jumped between angles—roulette wheels spinning, poker hands folding, bored guests checking watches.

Then, he stopped. His brows twitched as the image shifted.

Parker. Dead asleep on his office bearskin rug like some gluttonous Roman emperor who'd passed out mid-orgy. An empty whiskey bottle rolled near his outstretched hand. Draped across him like a discarded robe, a nude blonde woman slept against his back, her skin pale and unblemished under the soft overhead light.

Logan tilted his head.

The woman stirred.

She lifted her head, groggy at first, then alert. Still facing away from the camera, she slipped free of Parker's drunken embrace and tiptoed across the room. Logan's gaze sharpened as she moved toward the wall safe—its door left carelessly ajar. Her hesitation lasted only a second.

With sharp, deliberate hands, she grabbed Parker's sport bag from a nearby chair and stuffed it with thick stacks of bound hundred-dollar bills, her fingers working fast, yet mindful. Every few moments, she glanced back at Parker, who snored on, oblivious.

Then she turned.

Her face filled the monitor frame.

Logan sat back in his chair, Scotch forgotten.

"Cindy," he muttered. "Damn."

The cool composure he wore like tailored armor cracked—but it was there. He leaned forward again and continued to watch. Cindy finished dressing in a rush, yanking on her skirt and blouse, stuffing her underwear into her purse, stepping into her heels. With one final look at Parker, passed out on the floor, she slipped out the door and disappeared.

Logan's finger hovered over the keyboard. He switched to another feed—this one from the main gambling floor. Cindy appeared on the screen talking with two men Logan didn't recognize.

She was smiling that slow, knowing smile she only used when she was closing in on something. Her hand rested lightly on the taller man's forearm, her body angled just enough to draw him in without being obvious. It was an old move—refined, practiced. He'd seen her use it a dozen times before. On other marks. On him, once.

Another feed. Now Cindy and one of the men again—walking together through the lobby, a briefcase in the man's hand.

Logan's eyes followed them frame by frame. No hesitation. No looking back.

He paused the feed, then reached for the Scotch and took a slow, deliberate drink. The warmth traveled down his throat but did nothing to ease the sense of betrayal that coiled in his chest. Not because of love. That had never been part of the equation.

But control—that, she had just disrupted.

The room was silent except for the low hum of electronics. Snoop, his gray tabby, leapt onto his lap, curling into a purring crescent. Logan didn't flinch. He stroked the cat absentmindedly, eyes still on the frozen frame of the man and Cindy heading for the exit.

"That should bring in a nice piece of cash," he murmured, swirling the Scotch in his glass. "Our retirement to Geneva is within reach. Yes, indeed it is."

He leaned back again, calm restored, the calculations already forming behind his eyes. If Cindy thought she could outplay him—she hadn't been paying attention.

Not nearly enough.

He clicked back to the hallway footage. Rewatched her pass the briefcase off like it was routine. Smooth. Elegant. A perfect handoff.

She knew the cameras were there. That was the part that stung. She wasn't hiding from him. She was *challenging* him.

Logan took another drink.

He didn't believe in anger. Anger made your hand shake when it should be steady. Made you aim at the wrong person, or worse, the right one too soon. But disappointment—now that, he trusted. Disappointment never clouded his vision. It clarified it.

He reached over to the desk and tapped a few keys. The screen split—showing simultaneous feeds from the lobby, the garage, and the private elevator that led to Parker's offices.

Still nothing.

But it was only a matter of time.

Snoop purred louder, his head nudging Logan's wrist.

"You liked her too, didn't you?" Logan said. "Always sat in her lap when she visited. But then, you never did have a nose for disloyalty."

The cat blinked.

Logan set the glass down, Scotch half-finished. He didn't need it. Not now.

He opened a drawer beside him and pulled out a plain black notebook—small, worn, no markings on the cover. Inside were just names. Dates. Clean print, black ink, no flourishes. The kind of ledger that didn't go in the cloud. The kind you could burn in under five seconds.

He flipped to the newest page and wrote one word: *CINDY*

He paused. Then underlined it once.

No question marks. No notes.

He closed the book, returned it to the drawer, and locked it.

Outside, the city pulsed with neon. People winning and losing everything in minutes, thinking they were making choices. Logan knew better. The game was always rigged—it was just a matter of who placed the rigging first.

He gave Snoop one last scratch behind the ears and stood.

"Time to reset the board," he said.

The cat meowed once and jumped down, curling beneath the desk.

Logan pulled his jacket from the back of the chair and slid it on. Then he turned off the monitors one by one, the feeds vanishing into darkness like rooms going dead.

All except one.

The elevator.

Still waiting.

# CHAPTER 23

Parker sat behind his expansive mahogany desk, a cigar clamped between his teeth, its thick smoke curling toward the ceiling in lazy spirals. The office was dim except for the pale glow of the surveillance monitor in front of him. He narrowed his eyes at the screen and leaned closer, zooming in on one of the faces in the crowd.

Dave.

The man sat at a blackjack table in the casino below, a drink in one hand, chips in the other, completely unaware of the watchful eyes above.

Parker's lips curled into something between a sneer and a smirk. He picked up the phone and dialed.

Across town, Logan sat in his apartment, the light from his own monitor casting a pale hue over his sharp features. He was in the middle of a sandwich—pastrami on rye, the good kind from the deli on Fremont. The phone rang. He wiped his fingers on a napkin and answered.

"Hello," Logan said, taking another bite, chewing lazily.

Parker's voice came sharp and tense through the line. "One of the men on the tape—he's here. He's in the casino right now."

Logan didn't flinch. "My plan," he said flatly, "is to get them all together."

"You've got him now. Why wait?"

Logan's chewing slowed. There was a long pause before he replied, his tone cool, clipped. "I don't need instruction from you on how to do my job. Let me do it—or find someone else."

Without waiting for a response, Logan hung up.

Back in the office, Parker yanked the cigar from his mouth and stared at the dead receiver. He slammed it down and leaned back, irritation etched deep into the lines of his face.

"Arrogant jerk," he muttered, the cigar clamped once more between his teeth. He puffed, smoke billowing as the image of Dave on the screen continued to flicker.

The game had started, and now all he could do was wait for Logan to play his hand.

⚬

Dave was riding the high. Blackjack had been good to him that evening. He leaned back in his seat, his freshly won chips stacked like little towers of luck, and he adjusted the black fedora on his head with theatrical flair. It was his favorite—sleek, felted, and just flamboyant enough to draw attention without making him look like a magician. The dealer gave him a polite nod as he pushed in another pile of chips.

"Color me out," Dave said, pocketing his winnings with a grin that could split a poker table.

He sauntered away from the table, weaving through the neon-drenched chaos of the Venetian casino. The lights danced overhead, glinting off mirrors and slot machines, casting electric shadows across the floor. Music pulsed through the air, and Dave, feeling lucky and just a little drunk, locked eyes with a tall brunette draped in a silver cocktail dress.

She was stunning. Statuesque. Eyes like polished glass. Her lips curled in a half-smile as Dave approached.

"Hello, doll," he said, his voice velvet and swagger. "Want some company?"

His eyes traveled the length of her body like a slow elevator. She let him look, to a point.

"Only if you've got one grand, daddy," she said, chin tilted with professional disinterest.

Dave barked a laugh. "One grand? Can I be your daddy for free?"

The woman's expression flattened instantly. Her smile vanished behind the practiced disdain of someone who'd heard far worse. She pivoted on a sharp heel and glided away without another word.

Dave watched her go, still grinning. "One grand. What a joke," he muttered, mostly to himself.

His buzz carried him through the casino until he stumbled into the men's room—white tile, chrome, and the faint scent of too much air freshener. He ambled into a stall, not noticing the expensive leather shoes just one stall over. A man stood there in silence—unmoving.

Oblivious, Dave began to hum an old Sinatra tune while doing his business. His humming echoed off the tiles, a cheerful counterpoint to the tension gathering beside him.

A moment later, Dave emerged and shuffled to the sink. The man in the adjacent stall didn't move—not until Dave turned on the faucet. Then, the stall door creaked open. A glint of black steel. A glimpse of matte metal against a dark suit. But Dave remained unaware, drying his hands with a paper towel, still humming.

A YOUNG BOY, no older than ten, burst into the restroom, oblivious and in a hurry. He darted into the stall Dave had just vacated. The man with the expensive shoes—Logan—hesitated, then stepped back into his stall and closed the door before the boy noticed the gun in his hand.

Logan waited.

Dave tossed the towel in the trash and walked out, none the wiser.

Logan exhaled. Close one.

He slipped the handgun back into the holster under his jacket and emerged from the stall. He was at the exit when he heard the rapid patter of sneakers behind him.

"Mister!" the young boy called.

Logan turned. The boy held up a piece of paper—creased, smudged, crumpled. Logan's stomach tightened.

"You dropped this!"

Logan looked down. His hit list. Printed on unmarked paper in clean, block letters. Names of men and women, most crossed out in red pen. Brad Morgan. Dave Halpern. Cindy Walker.

Logan smiled tightly and took the paper from the boy's hand. "Yes. That's mine. Thank you."

The boy looked up at him with wide, earnest eyes. "Where are your parents?" Logan asked.

"Downstairs."

"You shouldn't talk to men you don't know," Logan said. "It's not safe."

"I just wanted to—"

"Run along," Logan interrupted, already folding the list and tucking it away inside his coat. "Find your parents."

The boy nodded and ran off, his shoes squeaking as he disappeared down the stairs.

Logan stood at the top of the mezzanine and turned to look over the railing. Below, the casino pulsed with light and motion—rows of flashing machines, laughter, the clang of jackpots, the dizzying dance of chaos. He scanned the floor.

No sign of Dave.

Logan narrowed his eyes and vanished in the crowd.

# CHAPTER 24

Cindy sat cross-legged on the edge of the hotel bed, her dark jeans tucked beneath her. Fully dressed, just like Brad, she leaned back on her hands, watching him with a half-smile. The open briefcase between them spilled over with neatly stacked bundles of hundred-dollar bills, like some fantasy scene from a heist film.

Brad scooped up a handful and fanned them out like playing cards.

"I've never—ever—seen this much money in my life," he said, his voice tinged with disbelief.

Cindy tilted her head, amused. "Ever? Ever, ever?" She grinned, drawing out the repetition with mock innocence.

He laughed, a little embarrassed. "I guess you have."

"Not this much," she admitted, reaching into the pile and flicking through the stacks. "But yeah... lots of cash. There's something hypnotic about it, isn't there?"

Brad tossed a few bundles into the air like confetti. They fluttered and landed on the bed, bouncing. For a brief moment, the stress left his face. He looked ten years younger.

"This money could change everything," he said, quieter now. "It'll pay off the loan shark, save the house, and—provide for my wife and her child."

"Her child?" Cindy's smile vanished. "You know, you really need to grow up. It's not all about you. Stop being a dick."

Brad's brows lifted. "A dick? Look, if your opinion mattered to me, I might be a little offended. But this is about a job. Afterward, you go your way, and I go mine."

Cindy shook her head, folding her arms. "If people had to be perfect before having kids, the species would've died out a long time ago."

"Can we not do this?" Brad muttered, rubbing his temples.

"'We' aren't doing anything," she said, her voice sharp now. "But I'm not going to sit here and let you act like you're the victim."

Brad's jaw tensed. "Everyone has a choice. My choice was not to become a father. Mary knew that. She still got pregnant. That's not a mistake—it's betrayal."

"You're selfish," Cindy said. "A good man, but selfish as hell."

Brad stood, pacing the room. "Selfish? Because I don't want to do to my son what my father did to me?" He turned to face her, eyes shadowed. "He walked out when I was five. Just disappeared. I don't want to be that guy."

"So what?" she snapped. "Move on."

There was silence. Then her voice softened, but it carried weight.

"I was raped," she said, looking down at her hands. "Years ago. I thought about abortion. Thought, 'How can I have this baby, this way?' I was broken. But she was still my blood. My daughter." Cindy looked up, eyes shimmering. "She's the best thing in my life. I've never regretted it. Not once."

Brad swallowed hard. "Cindy..."

"Forgive your wife," she said. "Forgive your father. We all screw up. We all hurt people. But what we do next... that's what matters."

"I know I've made mistakes," Brad said. He sat back down, quieter, as if the weight of her words had knocked the wind from him. "But being a father? I could ruin that kid."

"Yeah," she said with a shrug. "You might."

His eyes shot up. Unable to help himself, he grabbed a pillow and tossed it at her. It bounced off her shoulder. She hurled it right back, laughing, the heaviness between them lifting for a second.

Just then the door opened, and Dave stepped in, one hand still tugging off his fedora.

"Can we make this a party of three?" he said, eyeing the money on the bed with wide, greedy eyes.

The impromptu pillow fight came to a halt. Brad stood, all business again.

"Where the hell have you been?"

"The casino."

Brad moved toward him, his tone sharper now. "You're putting us all at risk. You could've been followed."

Dave waved his hand. "Don't worry. I was careful."

Brad didn't look convinced. Cindy, still seated on the bed, watched them both with a curious expression. Beneath her calm exterior, her mind was racing—about the money, the future, and the two men who had unknowingly placed their lives on the same ticking clock.

# CHAPTER 25

The sunlight bled through the blinds of Parker's Vegas office, casting angled slashes of light across the polished desk. Citrus and ink filled the air. Parker sat behind the desk in a leather chair, reclining as he sipped from a tall glass of orange juice and flipped through the morning paper. His fingers were stained with newsprint, but he didn't mind. This was his ritual—juice, silence, and a scan of the headlines before significant business of the day began.

A knock echoed against the heavy wood of the office door.

He didn't look up. "Come in."

The door creaked open, and two men stepped inside. No introductions, no words at first—just presence. The kind that turned a room cold. They wore no visible weapons, but they didn't need them. Their movements were deliberate, quiet. Controlled. Everything about them said they were professionals, the kind of men who didn't flinch when blood hit the floor.

The First Hit Man stepped forward, holding a folder thick with papers. "We have the background check you ordered on the two men conversing with Cindy in the casino."

The Second Hit Man glanced at his partner, then let out a short, amused chuckle. It wasn't warm. It wasn't kind. Just dark and knowing.

Parker lowered the newspaper. "What's so funny?"

The Second Hit Man leaned his weight to one side, smirking as though the punchline hadn't even landed yet. "You are not going to like what's in those papers."

Parker narrowed his eyes. "You want to fill me in?"

The First Hit Man didn't crack a smile. "It's not good."

Parker leaned forward now, his patience thinning. "What the hell is it?"

The Second Hit Man didn't blink. "You hired Logan to kill his own son."

The words froze the room. Parker stared at them, trying to process. "What?" he barked. "Give me that!"

He snatched the folder from the First Hit Man, nearly tearing the paper in his grip. His eyes darted over the contents, scanning page after page—photos, names, records, everything aligning in a grotesque coincidence. He didn't speak, didn't even breathe. Then, with a growl of frustration, he slammed the folder down on the desk so hard it shook the orange juice glass.

"Damn! Does he know?"

The Second Hit Man shook his head. "No. He has no clue."

Parker exhaled hard and dragged a hand over his scalp, fingers pausing at the crown of his head as if trying to press the truth back into his skull. He turned toward the window, staring out as though the view could offer some kind of solution. But the Vegas skyline didn't care.

"This has to be handled in a delicate way," he muttered. "Damn!"

Behind him, the Second Hit Man shifted his weight. "What did you have in mind?"

Parker didn't turn around. His voice grew colder. "Work together. Take them out and bring me my money. No one steals from me and lives."

The room went still for a moment before the Second Hit Man asked, quieter now, "You want us to kill Logan too?"

That made Parker face them. He turned, the lines in his face more defined, shadowed by the weight of what he was ordering.

"I don't have a choice," he said flatly. "He may eventually discover that the hit is on his son, and then he will be after me."

The First Hit Man raised an eyebrow, half-cocked with suggestion. "You could just retrieve your money and let everyone live. You know, live, and let live."

Parker didn't laugh. Instead, he opened a drawer in his desk and pulled out a cigar—thick, brown, Cuban. He clipped the end, lit it with a flick of his gold-plated lighter, and took a slow, measured drag. Smoke curled into the air between them, thin and white.

He glanced at the First Hit Man with something that might have been a smirk—or a warning.

"Where's the fun in that?"

Parker let the words settle in the space between them, the smoke from his cigar curling up like a question the other man would never be allowed to answer. He leaned back in his chair, the leather creaking just enough to remind the room to whom it belonged.

The First Hit Man—mid-thirties, lean, eyes too intelligent for someone who took orders—didn't flinch. But his smile faded. He stood with the weight of a man who'd killed before, probably often, probably clean. Still, he wasn't used to being invited and insulted in the same breath.

Parker liked that.

"I take it you don't do this for sport," the man said. "So what is it? Power? Ego?"

Parker tapped ash into the tray without looking away. "Control."

The man gave a slow nod, as if that explained everything. It almost did.

"Vegas is full of people who want things," Parker continued, voice smooth, rich with satisfaction. "They come here thinking luck is a currency. That desperation is private. But you and I? We know the truth. It's always a trade. Every table. Every bed. Every grave."

The man's gaze flicked toward the desk drawer Parker had opened earlier, the same one now holding more than cigars.

"You want all three," he said.

Parker smiled, cigar perched between his fingers. "Now you're starting to get it."

Outside, a siren wailed, muffled by the thick double-paned glass. Parker turned to look out over the Strip—over the blinking neon and anonymous sins beneath him.

"You're sure this Logan won't flinch?" the hit man asked.

Parker's eyes didn't leave the window. "Logan doesn't flinch. He calculates."

He turned back toward the man. "But he's been off. Ever since the job in New Mexico. Slower to act. Slower to clean. He's bleeding around the edges. That means it's time to test the center."

The man tilted his head. "And if he passes?"

Parker leaned forward now, eyes sharpened, no smile. "Then I sleep easier knowing my leash still fits."

"And if he fails?"

Parker took a final drag and stubbed the cigar out hard, grinding the embers into a smear of ash. His fingers drummed twice against the glass edge of the tray.

"Then you'll be standing exactly where you need to be."

The silence stretched. The First Hit Man didn't ask what that meant. He nodded.

A silent agreement made, one neither would speak of again.

Parker stood, adjusted the cuffs of his suit jacket. "You'll trail him. Don't engage unless I say. And if he turns on me?"

He met the man's eyes with something colder than malice. Something bureaucratic.

"You finish it."

The man reached into his coat and slid on a pair of black leather gloves. "Understood."

Parker moved to the bar cart in the corner, poured two fingers of bourbon—not for himself, but as a ceremony—and let the ice settle like a quiet verdict. He didn't hand it over. Just let it sit between them, untouched.

As both men turned to leave, Parker called after the First Hit Man, not raising his voice.

"One more thing."

The man paused, hand already on the door.

Parker didn't move. "If Cindy's still breathing by the end of the week... kill her first."

A flicker of pause, just long enough to register.

The First Hit Man opened the door, and both shooters walked out, shutting the door with a loud bang.

Parker walked back to his desk drawer, pulled out a cigar, and leaned back in his plush office chair as if he were the Godfather himself.

# CHAPTER 26

Outside the Venetian Hotel, the morning sun bounced off the polished surface of Cindy's Porsche. Brad, Dave, and Cindy threw suitcases into the trunk. Snacks and water bottles were thrown into the back seat. Dave settled into the back seat with the briefcase pressed against his leg like a bodyguard. Brad took the passenger seat while Cindy slid behind the wheel and revved the engine. The car peeled away from the curb and merged onto the Vegas expressway with swift aggression.

Inside the car, Dave gripped the edge of his seat as the city blurred past them.

"Hey lady," Dave said, trying to keep his voice light, "could you slow down a little?"

Cindy didn't flinch. "Uh, no. I can't drive slow."

"Well, Brad can," Dave offered, gesturing toward the passenger seat.

"No one drives this car but me," she shot back, her tone flat and final.

Dave sighed, leaned back, and stared out the window. Brad gave a crooked smile, watching her hands work the wheel with surgical precision.

"I understand," he said. "I wouldn't want to share this bad puppy either."

Just then, the Porsche jolted violently as it was rammed from behind. All three were flung forward in their seats. Cindy's knuckles went white on the steering wheel as she fought to keep control. Brad twisted around in his seat and spotted a black Ferrari FF tailing them like a predator.

"That was no accident," he said tightly, his eyes locked on the mirror. Then he turned to Cindy. "Can you handle this?"

She flicked a glance at him, her voice sharp. "It's not like we can change drivers now. I got this."

The Porsche surged forward, weaving through traffic, Cindy's foot pressing the gas like a challenge. But the Ferrari stuck with them, inch for inch. Another slam from behind sent them skidding against the guardrail. Metal screamed. Sparks spat. But Cindy jerked the car back onto the road without missing a beat.

"Holy shit!" Dave yelled, bracing against the seat.

"Can't this car go any faster?" Brad demanded.

"I'm flooring it right now!" Cindy barked, her eyes locked on the road, jaw clenched.

Behind them, inside the black Ferrari, Logan reached into the glove box and pulled out a pistol. He rolled the window down, aimed, and fired at one of the Porsche's tires. The Ferrari fishtailed, scraping the guardrail, but Logan adjusted and fired again, this time hitting one of the tires.

The Porsche swerved, smoke curling from its front wheels before Cindy brought it to a screeching halt. Chaos unfolded behind them as cars swerved and braked to avoid the Porsche.

Logan brought the Ferrari to the shoulder, jumped out, and stalked toward them with his gun drawn. His face was unreadable. Cold. Professional.

"Everyone out! Now! And bring the briefcase," he ordered.

Dave opened the rear door with hesitation, but knowing he had no choice, he handed the briefcase to Logan.

"Cindy," he said, closing the case, "what were you thinking? How did you get involved in this mess?"

Cindy stepped forward, her voice dry. "You mean, how did I get them involved in my mess."

Logan looked at her, a tinge of sadness in his eyes. "You know Parker will kill you... We need to move this party."

He reached into his pocket, tossed the Ferrari keys to Brad, and pointed toward the car. "Get in the car."

No one argued. They moved fast, adrenaline still buzzing under their skin, and climbed into Logan's Ferrari.

Logan sat in the back seat of the Ferrari with a cold grip on his handgun, the barrel aimed just inches from Dave's head. The motion of the car barely rocked him; his aim didn't waver.

"I have a gun on you," Logan said calmly, almost lazily. "So don't try anything. Just one wrong move and your friends go on a long journey. You know what I mean?"

Brad kept his eyes on the road as he merged onto the expressway, but he flicked his gaze to the rearview mirror. The sight of that steel barrel pointed at Dave made his stomach twist. He swallowed hard and gripped the steering wheel tighter.

Beside him, Cindy lit a cigarette with a practiced flick of her lighter. She took a slow drag, then exhaled through her nose like it was just another Sunday drive. But the tension in her jaw betrayed her calm.

Dave, wedged in the back seat beside Logan, looked from the gun to Logan's impassive face. "Where are you taking us?" he asked, voice dry and shaking.

"Shut up!" Logan said, eyes never leaving the road ahead.

Brad tried, futilely, to appeal to reason. "You have the money. Let us go."

"You know that's not how it works," Logan replied.

Logan turned his stare on Cindy. His voice went sharp. "Why steal from Parker? You know better. I never would've taken you for a dumb blonde... but now?"

Cindy flicked ash out the window, her tone casual but her eyes sharp. "The cash was just... lying there."

Brad jumped in. "Look, man, we sell life insurance. We came here to gamble. We stumbled on this money. We aren't a threat to you."

"Of course you're not," Logan said dryly. "Take the next exit and make your first right."

Brad's fingers tightened on the wheel as he followed instructions. He took the exit ramp and slowed the Ferrari into the curve.

"Next left," Logan said. "Drive to the end of the street. It dead ends."

The neighborhood changed into unfamiliar ter. Buildings grew sparser. Chain-link fences and weeds replaced casinos and neon. Brad's foot hovered over the brake as the road narrowed.

He checked the mirror again, hoping to read something in Logan's face, but the man's expression was flat—professional. Logan met his gaze and shook his head.

"Don't even think about it."

The Ferrari rolled to a stop in front of a rusted chain-link fence surrounding an abandoned warehouse. Concrete cracked beneath the tires. Trash fluttered in the wind.

Logan leaned forward and tapped the back of Brad's seat with the barrel of his gun. "Get out. Slowly. You too, Cindy."

Cindy crushed the cigarette into the ashtray and opened her door.

"Parker doesn't have to know!" she said, her voice more desperate now.

Logan ignored her.

He grabbed Dave by the collar and yanked the man halfway out of the car, then reached into his jacket and pressed a small remote. A mechanical whir filled the air as the warehouse door began to rise, revealing a yawning darkness within.

"C'mon," Logan muttered, dragging Dave toward the opening as Brad and Cindy hesitated beside the car.

Whatever waited inside that warehouse—it wasn't good.

# CHAPTER 27

Inside the dim, echoing warehouse, Logan slammed a button beside the entrance. The massive steel door groaned shut behind them. But before the echo of its descent faded, a thunderous hail of gunfire rang out.

Bullets ricocheted. Everyone scattered.

Cindy shrieked as a round tore through her side. She collapsed onto the cold concrete, blood spreading beneath her.

Logan dropped to one knee and returned fire in the direction of the shooter. His first bullet found its mark—one of the shooters grunted, staggered, and dropped lifeless.

Dave yelped in pain, clutching his leg as blood pulsed between his fingers.

Brad dove toward the downed assassin, yanked the gun from his slackened grip, and rolled for cover.

Up above, another shadow moved.

Logan spotted the second figure darting along the upper-level catwalk. He squeezed off a shot.

Gunfire cracked back, barely missing Logan's head.

He fired again, advancing.

The second shooter leaned over the balcony. That was enough. Logan lined up the angle, squeezed the trigger, and put a bullet right between the man's eyes. The body flipped over the railing and crashed to the floor below with a sickening thud.

Breathing hard, Logan strode toward Brad, gesturing.

Brad stepped out from behind cover, holding the rifle he'd taken. He leveled it at Logan.

"Drop the gun," Brad ordered.

Logan scoffed. "Go ahead and shoot!"

"No one has to die," Brad said, voice straining.

Behind him, Dave screamed in agony. Brad's focus faltered.

In a blur, Logan spun into a roundhouse kick. The rifle flew from Brad's hands. Logan threw a punch, but Brad blocked it with his forearm. For a second, Logan looked intrigued.

Then came a back kick.

They clashed in a flurry of brutal strikes—expert blocks, low sweeps, and elbow counters. But Logan was stronger, more experienced. He eventually dropped Brad with a precise blow.

Logan retrieved the rifle and stood over him, breathing hard. "You're well-versed in Karate, I'm impressed."

Ignoring Logan, Brad dropped to his knees and scrambled across the blood-slick floor toward Cindy. Her blouse was drenched in deep red, the fabric clinging to her chest and stomach, soaked through with warm blood that was already beginning to cool. She lay on her side, barely conscious, her face pale and lips tinged blue. Each breath she took came shallow, erratic—like her lungs were folding in on themselves, struggling for one last bit of air. Panic gripped Brad's chest as he hovered over her, his trembling hands unsure where to touch, where to press, where to begin.

"Hang on, Cindy. You'll be fine," he whispered, the words catching in his throat. His voice cracked as he brushed damp strands of hair from her forehead. She was slipping, and he could feel it—like trying to hold water in his hands.

Her lashes fluttered weakly, and her lips parted as she mouthed something. "My daughter... my daughter."

Brad's heart twisted. The way she said it—so quiet, so final—hit harder than any bullet ever could. He nodded, trying to anchor her with his presence. "We're going to get help, hold on," he promised, even though the words felt like lies the second they left his mouth.

"I'm so cold. I..." Her voice faded, trailing off like a fading echo.

"I'll keep you warm!" Brad shouted louder than he meant to, as if volume alone could drag her back from the brink. He leaned over her and began rubbing her arms up and down with both hands, frantic and desperate, the friction doing little against the chill that had already set into her skin. He could feel her slipping further away by the second, and he couldn't stop it. His breath came in gasps. He clung to her like a man dangling from a cliff.

But then—her eyes rolled back, slow, and final. Her chest stilled. There was no more breath. No more trembling. Just silence.

Brad froze. He sat there, motionless, hands still on her arms. The weight of the moment sank into him like a stone dropped into a lake. A heavy stillness settled in the room, broken only by the distant creak of the building and the quiet inrush of his ragged breathing. Then, after a long beat, he reached forward and closed her eyes with his fingertips, his touch trembling.

Without speaking, he pulled a nearby blanket over her body, careful to cover her up with reverence, as though tucking her in for sleep. His face was streaked with tears now, but he didn't bother to wipe them away—until finally, he used the back of his hand to drag them from his cheeks. He didn't sob. He didn't speak. He just sat beside her, broken until a groan pierced the air. He stood and stumbled toward Dave, who was pale and groaning.

"Dave! Were you hit?"

"My leg."

Brad tore off his shirt and wrapped it around the wound, trying to stem the bleeding. He looked up at Logan.

"If you're going to shoot, then do it. Or leave us be."

Logan crossed the room, glanced down at the first shooter, then shook his head. "That damn Parker," he muttered. "Son of a bitch is trying to kill me too."

He collected the pistols from both fallen men and carried them to a nearby table. Turning to Brad and Dave, he barked, "Get over here. Now!"

"He can't walk!" Brad snapped.

"Get him over here—or walking will be the least of his problems."

Brad didn't argue. He dragged Dave by the arm toward the table, ignoring his friend's howl of pain. Then he returned, picked up the briefcase and slammed it onto the table. He collapses into a chair beside it, shoulders sagging.

"Open it up," Logan commanded.

Brad obeyed. Logan counted the cash in silence, then snapped the case shut.

He shook his head. "You've seen me. And you know how this works."

Brad looked up, eyes red. "We're just a couple of ordinary people from an ordinary town. We haven't seen anything."

"Of course you haven't," Logan said. He motioned toward Brad. "Get your friend's wallet from his pocket and put it on the table. I need yours too—your cell phones. I like to know who I'm killing. It's a character flaw."

Brad reached into Dave's pants and pulled the wallet free. Dave flinched in pain. Brad then tossed his own wallet next to it.

Logan picked up Dave's first. He flipped through it—a photo of a woman, another of aging parents, a Hamilton & Haines employee ID, credit cards, and a strip club membership.

"Strip club?" Logan asked with a crooked grin.

He tossed the wallet back to Dave.

He took Brad's next. Inside, he found a photo of a woman and a little boy. He held it up.

"You know this boy personally?"

"Yes," Brad replied, voice low. "That's me."

Logan froze.

His hand trembled.

He turned away, sweat beading on his brow. His body rocked, as if on unstable ground. He took a long, ragged breath and tried to compose himself.

He placed the photo down and staggered into a chair.

"I occasionally have military flashbacks," he said, voice distant. "They can be hell."

"You served?" Brad asked. "Now you're a killer?"

"Combat is killing," Logan said. "We killed people. Some were innocent... others, not so much."

He glanced at Brad's employee ID.

"You work at Hamilton & Haines?"

"I mentioned that before."

Logan stared. "Any kids to be orphaned today?"

"No kids."

Dave grimaced. "His wife... she's pregnant. With their first child."

"Dave, shut up!" Brad snapped.

But Logan wasn't listening to him anymore. His face softened. The hard exterior cracked just a little.

"I'm tempted to kill you right now," Logan murmured. "But today is your lucky day. I've filled my quota."

He stood up, all business again.

"Tomorrow... who knows. I've got urgent business to take care of. Move it. We're going to the upper level."

Brad got under Dave's arm and helped him up. Logan pocketed the phones and wallets, then motioned toward the nearby freight elevator, a gun still trained on them.

They stepped inside. The doors clanged shut.

Inside the dim warehouse elevator, the metal doors slid open with a groan. The space beyond was bleak, industrial, and stripped bare, like a forgotten relic of violence and secrets. Logan gestured forward with a curt nod, keeping his gun low but ready. Brad helped Dave to his feet and guided him out of the elevator and into the room ahead.

The tenth floor of the warehouse was a vast, concrete expanse. Harsh fluorescent lighting buzzed above. The odor of oil and damp insulation pervaded the air.

Brad helped Dave ease down onto the air mattress with care, trying not to jostle his friend's injured leg. Dave gritted his teeth, groaning. Brad straightened up and turned to face Logan.

"Can't we negotiate this?" Brad asked, his voice dry with desperation.

Logan stood with one shoulder against the doorframe, arms crossed loosely across his chest. His face was unreadable.

"What do you have to negotiate with?" Logan asked. Brad exhaled, swallowing his pride.

"Nothing... I have nothing to offer. I... I have a wife... she holds my heart." He hesitated, then looked Logan square in the eyes. "And she's having my baby."

Logan stared at him for a beat, unmoved. "Don't cry me a river," he muttered.

Without another word, Logan stepped out of the room and shut the heavy steel door behind him. A loud click followed—he had locked them in.

Outside, Logan stood alone in the narrow hallway for a moment. His mask of cruelty cracked. He winced, the weight of what he'd just done sinking in for a flicker of a second. But almost immediately, he straightened up, shook it off, and stepped back into the elevator. The doors hissed shut.

❖

Across town, at the top of a towering high-rise that served as Parker's lair of corruption, the elevator doors opened again. Logan stepped out, striding toward Parker's office like a man on a mission. There was no hesitation in his walk. This wasn't a visit—it was a reckoning.

He didn't bother knocking politely. He banged on the door once, then pushed it open at Parker's grunt of "Come in."

As always, Parker lounged at his desk like a smug king, a thick cigar smoldering between his fingers. He was known not to look up when his guests arrived. After all, he had the best security and a swollen ego. That changed when Logan entered and pulled a gleaming .357 Magnum from beneath his coat. He raised it and aimed it straight at Parker's face.

Parker's eyes widened. He reached for the hidden panic button behind his desk, but Logan took a step forward and pressed the gun barrel against Parker's forehead.

"You'll be dead long before you reach that button," Logan warned.

Parker froze.

"What do you want, Logan?"

Logan's eyes, burning with betrayal, didn't lower the gun. If anything, he pushed it harder into Parker's skull.

"You sent your goons to kill me," Logan said through clenched teeth. "I've been your right-hand man for years, and this is how you repay me?"

Parker shrugged stiffly, trying to maintain composure. "Either I kill you or wait for you to kill me... easy choice."

Logan's jaw tightened. His knuckles whitened around the grip of the gun.

"He's my son, asshole! Why didn't you just call the whole thing off? You don't even need the damn money."

Parker exhaled smoke and said, "Don't need the money? You're getting soft. This isn't about cash, Logan. It's about respect. My men look up to me. You think I can let people steal from me and live? The situation has gotten out of hand."

Logan's voice dropped to a deadly hush. "My son is expecting his first child. You wanted me to kill my only child?"

He moved the gun lower, shoving it beneath Parker's chin, forcing his head to tilt back.

"Tell me why I shouldn't just splatter your brains all over this nice mahogany."

Parker flinched. His mouth twitched. He hesitated.

"He's your estranged son," Parker said. "You didn't raise him. You really don't have a relationship."

Logan's eyes narrowed.

"He's my blood, you son of a bitch."

With a sudden burst of rage, Logan whipped the butt of the gun across Parker's temple. Parker cried out and collapsed to the floor, clutching his head.

Groaning, Parker struggled to his feet, wobbling as blood trickled down his temple.

"Calm down," he panted. "We can work this out."

Logan lowered the gun and turned away, heading toward the door.

"No, Parker," he said coldly. "We cannot."

He raised the weapon again, aiming directly at Parker's heart.

Parker flinched and threw up a hand in desperation. "Don't be stupid! You shoot me, your son dies!"

Logan stopped, his finger tightening on the trigger.

"What the hell are you talking about?"

Parker's lips curled into a smug smile. He straightened, despite the pain.

"Remember that job in Chicago?" he asked. "The one you turned down?"

Logan narrowed his eyes. "What about it?"

Parker's gaze dropped to his watch. "Your son—your sweet little small-town gambler who owes me money? I had one of my men insert a body cavity bomb in him. It's set to go off in..." He checked the time again. "...about forty-five minutes. You shoot me, and my men will make it go off. KABOOM."

Logan's breath caught. His hand trembled, rage boiling inside him.

"You son of a bitch," he growled.

Parker smirked. "It's not personal."

Logan turned, storming out of the room. This wasn't over—not by a long shot.

# CHAPTER 28

Logan's black Ferrari tore along Interstate 215 East, its engine roaring like a beast unchained. His hands gripped the wheel tightly, knuckles white, eyes locked straight ahead. Every second that ticked by was a countdown to death for Brad. He had forty-five minutes, maybe less. Sweat traced lines down Logan's temples despite the AC blasting. He didn't even blink.

As the Vegas skyline blurred past, he swung off the highway and screeched into the industrial lot in front of the warehouse. The tires barked against the pavement as he slammed the car into park. Without bothering to shut the door, Logan leapt out, sprinted to the metal panel, and punched the button to raise the warehouse door.

The massive steel slab groaned and lifted. Logan ducked beneath it before it fully cleared the frame and rushed inside. His boots echoed harshly across the concrete floor as he crossed to the freight elevator. He hit the button for the tenth floor with the flat of his palm, panting now. Tense. The walls of the elevator hummed and creaked on its slow rise.

When the doors slid open, Logan stepped into the tenth-floor corridor, eyes narrowed, instincts sharp. Something felt off—quieter than it should have been. Too quiet.

He slid his hand into his coat and drew his pistol with practiced ease. The cold steel felt natural in his grip. He advanced, slow and measured, down the dim hallway, every sense alert. The air felt thick, almost electric. He reached the door to the room where he had left Brad and Dave. The steel door stood closed, but he noticed it—ajar.

Logan's jaw clenched.

He raised the gun, kept his body low, and moved closer.

Logan crouched just outside the door, his back pressed to the wall. A faint scuffling sound reached his ears—then a sharp, wet *smack*. He edged forward, peering through the narrow gap in the door. Inside, a man held a pistol on Brad and Dave. The shooter was tall, wiry, and cruel-looking, and he delivered a fierce backhand across Brad's face.

"You need to tell me where the money is," the man snarled. "Or we're going to have a long and painful night."

Brad's lip bled, but he didn't flinch. He looked the shooter dead in the eye.

"We don't have the money," Brad said hoarsely. "It was taken from us by another guy. He had a gun, he took it—there's nothing here. How many times will you not get it?"

Another *crack!* The shooter slapped him again, harder this time. Brad's head snapped to the side.

"Punk," the man growled. "You think I won't shoot? You think—"

A whistling sound cut through the air like a ghost.

*Thunk!*

Logan's blade embedded in the side of the man's neck with a sickening crunch. The shooter's eyes widened in shock. Blood sprayed from the severed artery as he stumbled back, clutching his throat. He fell like a dropped marionette, twitching once before going still.

Logan stepped into the room, his expression blank, and calmly retrieved the knife. He wiped it on the dead man's shirt before walking to the small sink in the corner. Without a word, he dropped the blade into it. The metallic clatter echoed through the room.

Dave, still lying on the mattress, gawked. "You learn that in the military too?"

Logan didn't look at him. "Knife-throwing I learned from a friend I met at boot camp," he said, his voice low and emotionless. "Many years ago."

Brad sat up, rubbing his jaw. He stared at Logan with raw, bitter eyes. "Why didn't you just let him kill us?" he asked. "Maybe you're just reserving that pleasure for yourself."

Logan met his gaze, silent for a moment.

"I'm your father," he said.

Brad's voice came out in a raw, disbelieving rasp. "You've lost your mind. I have no father. I'm an orphan."

Logan didn't react with anger. Instead, he walked to the table and sat down, his eyes never leaving Brad. The room was dim and still heavy with tension. Logan extended a hand across the table and reached for Brad's. The gesture was strange—out of place amidst all the blood and betrayal. Brad jerked his hand away like he'd been stung.

Logan let his hand fall back to the table. He spoke in a hushed tone. "Your mother's name was Beverly. You were raised by your Aunt Mildred after I left... when you were five."

The words hit Brad like a slow-moving train. He jumped up, knocking over a metal lamp with a crash. It clattered across the floor. Logan stood too and instinctively moved toward him, arms extended. But Brad shoved him back hard in the chest.

Dave, watching from the mattress, looked like he'd just witnessed a ghost tear through the wall. His mouth hung open.

"You have no problem killing your own son?" Brad shouted, his voice trembling with fury.

"I didn't know," Logan said, his tone laced with guilt. "I won't shoot you."

Dave raised a hand weakly from the mattress. "What about me?"

Logan gave a dry exhale. "You get a pass too."

Dave let out an audible sigh and slumped back against the pillow, clutching his bandaged leg.

Brad's jaw was clenched tight. His hands were fists at his sides. "You've been in Vegas this whole time? You knew where I was. You could've called. You could've visited."

"And say what?" Logan's voice rose for the first time. "Say, 'Hey son, I decided to become a contract killer'? Say, 'I'm sorry I left you to be raised by someone else because I was too broken to stay'? I chose this life, Brad. I chose to leave you in better hands. There was nothing to say."

"Spare me," Brad growled. "I have a father who's not only a bastard—but a fucking killer, too."

"You can keep hating me," Logan said, eyes hard. "But right now, you need me."

"I don't need you," Brad snapped.

Logan stepped closer, his voice lowering again. "I know about the explosive."

Brad froze.

Dave sat up straighter, eyes darting between the two of them. "Let him help!"

Brad hesitated, breathing hard, his entire body coiled with distrust. Then something shifted in his expression. The bravado cracked.

"Do you still have the briefcase?" he asked.

Logan nodded. "I have the briefcase."

He gripped Brad by the shoulders, firm but not aggressive. For the first time, the assassin looked like something else, something human.

"You can't wait another minute," Logan said. "That bomb has to come out."

Dave tipped back the bottle of Jura Scotch and took a long, burning swig before slumping deeper into the mattress with a groan. He raised a hand casually in the air, as if interrupting a wedding toast.

"I hate to break up this love feast," he said, voice raspy and dry, "but I got a wife I need to get back to."

Both Brad and Logan turned their heads in his direction, startled by the outburst.

Dave shrugged, expression flat. "To divorce her... ya know."

Brad let out a weary breath and turned to Logan. "Just give me the damn briefcase. If I pay them, they won't detonate the bomb. That'll be the end of it."

Logan's jaw clenched. "End of it?" he spat. "How fucking naive."

Brad scoffed. "Your fatherly charm astounds me."

"Giving you that briefcase gets you killed," Logan said, his tone low and cold. "It's already killed Cindy. Time is running out. You need help—so lie down and shut the fuck up!"

Brad's chest rose and fell with sharp, shallow breaths. He looked at Dave. Their eyes locked.

"Do it," Dave said. "You don't have a choice. I can't fix it."

Brad's voice lowered. "How will you take it out?"

"The same way it was put in," Logan replied. "I'll have to cut you. It's the only way."

A long silence filled the room. Then Brad asked, "How can I trust you?"

"You can't," Logan said flatly. "Never trust anyone... not even your friends."

Logan stood up but didn't move right away. He gave Brad a moment, a space to flinch, to lash out, to bolt. But Brad just stood frozen, his fists twitching with indecision.

Logan turned and walked toward the doorway. Dave after him, pulled him aside, and whispered under his breath, "Give him a little time... He needs to adjust."

Behind them, Brad paced in a tight circle. His mind raced. His gut twisted. His instincts screamed at him.

"Maybe there's no bomb anyway," he muttered. "Maybe it's just a huge fucking joke. Big Rob wants me to freak out."

Logan turned his head just enough to answer. "Maybe. Do you want to take that risk?"

Dave laughed—short, dry, almost fond. "He's a true gambler," he said. "A terrible gambler, but a true gambler."

Brad shot him a sideways glare. "Thanks for the compliment."

"Just keeping it real, my brother."

Brad exhaled through his nose. A long pause.

Resigned, bitter, and scared—he said, "Okay. Let's do it."

Brad peeled off his shirt and tossed it aside. The stale air of the tenth-floor room hit his bare skin, cold and indifferent. He lay back on the air mattress with a resigned exhale. Every muscle in his body tensed. Across the room, Logan walked to the sink, turned on the water, and rinsed the blood from the blade he'd used earlier. The metal glinted under the dull warehouse lighting.

Without a word, Logan reached into his backpack and pulled out a familiar bottle—the Jura Scotch. He held it up.

"You want a drink before we start?" he asked.

Brad glanced at the bottle and managed a weak grin. "Jura? Damn straight."

Logan looked at Dave. "Dave?"

"Absolutely," Dave replied, his voice tight with pain but hopeful for any kind of distraction.

Logan opened a cabinet and retrieved three dusty glasses. He poured three fingers of Scotch into each and handed them out—one to Brad, one to Dave, and he kept the last for himself.

Before the first incision, Logan crouched beside Dave and examined the wound on his leg. It was still bleeding, the improvised bandage already soaked. He poured a splash of Jura into the wound.

Dave cried out in agony. "Jesus Christ!"

"It hurts," Logan said evenly, "but it'll help save your leg."

Logan scanned the room. He found an old sheet from a torn mattress in the corner and sliced it into long strips. Then he ducked below the sink and pulled out a roll of duct tape. Working fast, he wrapped the strips around Dave's leg and secured them with layers of tape. Still, the bleeding continued, dark and stubborn.

"You need a tourniquet," Logan muttered.

He dug around until he found a worn leather belt in an old duffel bag. He tightened it around Dave's upper thigh until the blood slowed to a trickle. Dave gasped, biting his lip.

Logan gave his shoulder a brief pat, then moved to Brad.

Kneeling beside him, Logan studied the small scar low on Brad's abdomen—the faint, unnatural ridge that marked where the device had been planted. He unscrewed the cap on the Scotch and poured a thin stream directly onto the area.

Brad screamed, the sound sharp and raw.

"Hold still," Logan said, his tone soft but firm.

He pressed the blade to the skin and began to cut. The knife slid in deliberately. Brad clenched his jaw until his teeth ached. Sweat poured from his forehead.

Logan worked in silence, slicing three inches along the tissue. Blood welled up along the cut, pooling across Brad's side. Another scream tore from his throat.

"Almost there," Logan muttered, eyes narrowing as he angled the blade deeper.

# CHAPTER 29

The living room glowed beneath the amber hue of a corner lamp. Mary sat curled on the plush gray sofa, legs tucked beneath her, a heavy photo album spread across her lap. Her fingers moved over the glossy images—frozen moments from their Hawaiian wedding. She smiled at each memory: the hibiscus tucked in her hair, the way Brad grinned at her in his linen suit, the blue waves crashing behind them like applause from the gods.

She lingered on one photo longer than the rest—Brad carrying her across the sunlit sand. A small, wistful laugh escaped her lips.

After a long moment, she closed the album and rose from the sofa. She walked it back to the bookshelf, sliding it neatly into its place. As she reached down to adjust a row of children's books on the bottom shelf, her fingers brushed against something sticking out from a worn hardcover. Curious, she pulled the book free and saw the edge of a folded letter protruding like a forgotten whisper.

Mary plucked the letter loose and opened it. She was careful not to tear the fragile paper.

*Dear Dad,Whereber you are, I want you to know I luv you and miss you soo much. Aunt Mildred is cool and she is a realy realy good cook, but I would like to see you Dad. Can you come home? You could help me with my math homework. Mr. Grimes is really, really mean. an father and son day is coming and it would be super if you and me can go. Say you will come. Please Dad! I luv you.Brad*

Mary stared at the letter, her breath caught somewhere between her chest and throat. A tear welled up, then rolled down her cheek as she folded the letter and held it against her heart.

---

Elsewhere in the city, in a dim bedroom drenched in low, sensual light, Lindsey lay tangled in crimson sheets, her back arched, eyes closed in release. A young man—no older than twenty-five, with tousled black hair and a lean, athletic frame—collapsed beside her, chest heaving. Their bodies slick with sweat, they melted into each other's arms like two fires just burned out.

She traced a finger down his chest, smiling lazily.

"God, you're better than my husband ever was," she whispered.

The young lover chuckled and kissed her shoulder.

"I bet he doesn't even know what he's missing."

Lindsey smiled again, but this time, it didn't quite reach her eyes.

The young man propped himself up on one elbow, his gaze drifting lazily across Lindsey's face. There was a sly smile tugging at the corner of his lips as he asked, "When did you say your husband will be home?"

Lindsey, still stretched out on the bed, her dark hair fanned across the pillow, gave a nonchalant shrug. "I'm not sure," she said, voice light and unconcerned. "Does it matter?"

He tilted his head, studying her with playful wariness. "You're dangerous," he murmured, reaching to caress the curve of her waist. His fingers traced her skin like he was writing secrets on parchment. "Do you get off on him catching us?" He dipped lower, brushing a kiss just above her hip. "Does it make you horny?"

She chuckled, but it carried no amusement. "Maybe it makes *you* horny."

He smirked. "He doesn't make that body sing like I do, does he?"

Lindsey's eyes flicked toward the ceiling. Her smile flattened. "Why are we talking about my husband?" she asked, voice cool and edged with irritation. She grabbed him by the hair, yanking his attention back to her. "Your job is to take my mind *off* my husband."

His grin returned, devilish and eager. "At your service, Madame."

He began to move down between her thighs, his mouth trailing slow kisses down her belly. Lindsey turned her face away, eyes settling on the far wall. The wallpaper there was torn at the corner, and she stared at it, her expression unreadable.

As the young man continued southward, Lindsey drew in a long, shaky breath—her inhale sharp, almost bracing. But even as her body responded, she thought of Dave and what could have been.

⚍◆⚎

Mary lay against a stack of pillows, her body relaxed beneath a floral comforter as she flipped a page in her romance novel. The bedroom was quiet—too quiet—and the words on the page had begun to blur into one another. With a sigh, she closed the book and reached for her phone on the nightstand.

She tapped Brad's name and held the phone to her ear.

It rang once. Then his voice came through, detached and familiar.

*"This is Brad, leave a message."*

Mary didn't bother. She hung up without a word.

The phone sagged in her hand as she stared at the ceiling. After a moment, she set it aside and picked the novel back up, flipping to the last page she'd read. But her eyes barely scanned the first sentence before she dropped it again with a frustrated huff.

She pushed the covers off and rose from the bed. Barefoot, she padded across the room and stepped into the adjoining bathroom. The soft hum of the house closed in around her.

As she reached for the sink, her breath hitched.

A sharp tug bloomed in her abdomen.

She looked down, startled. A warm trickle ran down the inside of her thigh. Within seconds, a stream followed, forming a small glistening puddle on the tiled floor.

"Oh…" she whispered, her hand pressing against the curve of her belly.

She left the bathroom and crossed to the bed. Her fingers trembled as she grabbed her phone. She scrolled and tapped *Lindsey*.

The phone rang. Mary closed her eyes, bracing for what was next.

———◄O►———

The young lover was still nestled between Lindsey's thighs when her cell phone vibrated against the nightstand. She reached over with a lazy hand, her body still humming from his touch. The screen flashed *Mary*.

Without sitting up, she answered.

"Not a good time—" she began, her voice thick with post-pleasure haze.

Mary's voice came shaky and urgent through the receiver. "My water broke. Can you come over... please?"

Lindsey's expression shifted. She put a hand on the young lover's head, motioning for him to stop. Confused, he lifted his face. Mary turned away from him, focusing fully on the phone now.

"I'll be right there," she said, already swinging her legs over the edge of the bed. "Just relax."

She ended the call, tossed the phone aside, and stood completely naked.

The young lover propped himself on his elbow. "Is everything okay?"

"Yeah," Lindsey said, reaching for her clothes. "A friend needs me."

"Now?"

"Yes. Now."

She didn't explain further.

———◆———

The doorbell rang, and Mary descended the staircase, her hand pressed to her lower back. When she opened the front door, Lindsey stood there grinning with the kind of excitement that only a best friend could muster at a moment like this.

"I'm about to be a godmother! Me! This is so happening!" Lindsey declared, bouncing into the house.

Mary shut the door behind her, but Lindsey's smile faded when she took a good look at her friend. Mary's face was tight with worry, her posture hunched.

They crossed the living room and sat on the sofa.

"My water broke," Mary said, her breath shallow. "And I'm having contractions and they're close—"

"Did you time them?" Lindsey asked, already pulling her phone from her purse.

"Yeah, fifteen minutes apart."

"So why the sad face?"

"I can't reach Brad. Will you call Dave and find out what's going on?"

"Where are your bags?"

"Call Dave!"

Lindsey hesitated, making a face. "You know I hate calling Dave. I didn't want him getting the wrong idea... or even the right one... I'll call."

She sighed and pressed the contact on her phone. It rang once and went to voicemail.

"This is Dave. What the message?" came his recorded voice.

"It went straight to voicemail," Lindsey said, frowning. "The battery could be dead. He never keeps it charged—"

Before she could finish, Mary shot up from the sofa.

"I can't do this without Brad! I just can't! What am I going to do? We thought we had two more weeks, I—"

"I'm sure he's fine," Lindsey tried to say, stepping closer, but Mary kept going.

"Lindsey, I'm scared. He's in danger and I need him here. I can't do this without Brad, I can't!"

Lindsey grabbed her friend by the shoulders and gave her a little shake.

"You can! And damn it, you will! Listen, you are a strong woman. You don't need a man to make this happen."

Her voice softened. "Hey... you can do this. *We* can do this."

Mary turned away just then, clutching her belly as another contraction tore through her. She inhaled, deep breaths turning into quiet groans.

"We need to get you to the hospital," Lindsey said, reaching for her purse.

"I need my husband! Damn him!" Mary cried, nearly doubling over as wave after wave of pain seared through her body.

"This is not what we planned," she whimpered. "Brad should be here."

"He can't do shit for you right now," Lindsey said firmly. "He's not here... I'm here."

She glanced down at Mary—and froze.

A pool of blood had formed on the floor. Bright red. Spreading fast.

Lindsey rushed to her, panic rising in her throat. "My God, you're bleeding!"

Mary looked down, horror overtaking her features. The blood had soaked through the legs of her pants, dripping into puddles at her feet. She gasped, eyes wide, lips trembling.

"Lindsey..." she whispered, voice breaking.

"I've got you," Lindsey said, already reaching for her phone. "Just hold on, Mary. I've got you."

# CHAPTER 30

Logan let the bloody knife fall from his fingers. It clattered to the floor with a dull metallic thud. He grabbed the bottle of Jura Scotch and poured a generous amount over his hands, rubbing the alcohol into his skin like soap, as if it could cleanse not only the blood but the weight of what he was about to do.

He leaned over Brad again and began kneading the area around the implanted device, coaxing it to the surface with firm, practiced fingers. A small piece of metal emerged beneath the skin, a tiny, insidious shape embedded just under the flesh. Logan squinted, examining it.

"Amateurs," he muttered. "This is really shoddy... but still dangerous."

Brad tilted his head, sweat glistening on his brow. "Can you take it out?"

"I can take it out," Logan said, his tone steady but focused. "The trick is getting it out without it exploding. That's not so easy."

Brad's face tightened. "Maybe we should leave it alone."

Logan gave a soft snort. "No worries. I said it's not easy, I didn't say I couldn't do it."

He studied the tiny device, noting the colored wires tucked inside it—green, blue, red, and black—all converging toward a blinking red light. Logan turned and crossed the room to the sink. He dropped to one knee and opened the cabinet beneath. A moment later, he emerged with a small green toolbox.

Carrying it back to Brad, he flipped open the case and pulled out a tool that looked like a cross between tweezers and a scalpel—thin, sharp, precise. He crouched and lifted one of the wires, examining the way it looped and joined with the others.

Brad shifted. "Is there a problem?"

Logan didn't look up. "Just be still, son."

"Don't call me son," Brad said through gritted teeth. "I'm not your son."

Logan paused for a beat and looked at him.

"I was a lousy father, an absent father," he admitted. "You may hate me... but I'll always be your father."

He returned to the bomb, eyes narrowing.

"Real fathers don't leave," Brad shot back. "They provide. They're responsible—"

"I was responsible," Logan interrupted, his voice even. "Some times... sometimes you give more by leaving."

Without another word, he used the tool to disconnect the blue wire. Brad winced but said nothing. Logan's focus was unbreakable.

"These next ones are tricky," he murmured. "Please be still."

Brad gave a faint nod and held himself rigid, hardly breathing.

Logan's hand moved with calm precision. He snipped the red wire. Then the black. The blinking light ceased. He let out a long breath and withdrew the small device from Brad's side. Blood trickled from the incision, dark and thin, but the bomb—at least visually—looked disarmed.

And then it *ticked*.

A single sharp sound, mechanical and cold.

Everyone froze.

"Fuck!" Logan bellowed. He grabbed the device and dashed to the window. With one powerful motion, he hurled it outside.

It soared through the air and struck the hood of a parked Ferrari.

The car *exploded*.

The shockwave rattled the windows. Flames engulfed the vehicle; luckily, the street was empty.

Brad staggered to the window and looked down in disbelief.

Logan stood beside him, frowning at the carnage.

"Damn!" he growled. "It hit my car!"

Dave, still pale, sat against the wall and exhaled. "That was scary," he said. "What luck?"

No one answered.

Logan reached for the bottle of Jura Scotch. He held it up and said, "Here's to good ol' luck. May ye forever reign."

He took a long swig, then passed the bottle to Brad, who didn't hesitate. He chugged the liquor down in one smooth motion.

Brad stared at the shattered glass on the floor, his chest rising and falling with the weight of what had just happened.

"That could have been me..." he said, his voice raw. "In a thousand pieces, scattered—"

"It *wasn't* you," Logan snapped, cutting him off. He turned to face Brad, his expression torn somewhere between shame and fury.

"I deserve your hatred," Logan said. "For a long time, I hated myself."

Brad's voice cracked. "I was five years old. *Five*. You left me with Aunt Mildred. You said you'd be back—you were going to the store." His jaw tightened. "But you never came back."

Logan looked down, unable to meet his son's eyes. "I was just a kid myself," he said. "The grief... soul-crushing grief... day after day. Beverly loved me. And I failed her, even in death."

He turned toward the broken window, watching the fire crew swarm the wreckage of the exploded Ferrari below. The glow of the flames flickered against his face, and for a moment he looked as haunted as any ghost.

"Beverly paid the bills, cooked the food," he said. "She was the responsible one. She never made me feel bad because I didn't have a job..."

He stopped speaking and swallowed.

"I lost all sense of emotion and feeling. Killing became easy. And the money—" he gave a bitter laugh "—the money was good."

Brad's voice was sharp and cold. "Tell it to your priest. You have no idea how many nights I prayed for your return. The nightmares I had about Mom's burial. How could you do that to your *own son*? I—"

He stopped and looked over at Dave. Their eyes met, and something passed between them, it was either pain or understanding.

"It doesn't matter," Brad muttered. "I survived without you then, and I damn sho' don't need you now."

Logan didn't flinch. "I need your forgiveness," he said. "I am truly sorry."

Brad turned away and walked over to Dave. He knelt beside the mattress.

"Maybe you should try to hear him," Dave whispered.

"I *hear* him," Brad muttered back. "I don't forgive him."

Logan came closer and squatted beside them, his eyes unreadable. His voice was rough and low when he spoke.

"Every bullet I shot was money for your food," he said. "Every bomb I detonated helped you have a very Merry Christmas. Every damn throat I cut paid for your education."

He looked down, unable to meet Brad's gaze.

"I won't apologize for surviving," Logan said. "But I'm sorry I wasn't there."

Brad clenched his jaw. "That five-year-old boy only wanted his Dad. That's all he wanted! That's what he asked Santa for—a *Dad*."

He stood and started pacing for a moment before facing Logan again.

"Are we done here?" he snapped. "Dave has a bullet in his leg that needs to come out."

Logan gave a faint shake of his head. "Actually, the bullet went through his leg. He'll be fine."

"Are you going to give me the briefcase or not?" Brad demanded. "I need to go home to my wife. And so does Dave."

Dave let out a dry chuckle. "Speak for yourself," he said. "My wife don't exactly make me wanna come home."

Logan walked over to the table, lifted the briefcase, and opened it. He peeked inside, then clicked it shut again and carried it over.

There's more than enough there to pay off the loan sharks and live comfortably. But I'll hold onto it until you're safely on that plane headed for home."

Logan looked around the room, the silence thick between them. The chaos of the world outside raged on—but inside, something fragile and unresolved still lingered in the air.

Logan's eyes swept the room once more, then he looked at the others.

"We need to get out of here," he said, his tone brisk and sharp.

He turned to Dave. "Can you walk?"

Dave winced as he shifted his leg. "Do I have a choice?" he said, forcing a smirk. "Let's do this."

The three of them—Logan, Brad, and Dave—left the warehouse behind, stepping into the cool night air. The city buzzed in the distance, but this part of town was quiet, abandoned, waiting.

As they walked down the cracked sidewalk, they spotted a yellow cab idling at the corner, its driver leaning against the hood, sipping coffee from a Styrofoam cup. Without hesitation, Logan stormed toward the vehicle.

He walked straight up to the driver, grabbed him by the collar, and yanked him away from the cab with alarming force. The coffee cup flew from the man's hand and landed on the pavement. Logan shoved the driver to the ground without saying a word. The man hit the concrete with a grunt and scrambled in surprise.

Logan, Brad, and Dave piled into the cab. Logan slid behind the wheel, slammed the door, and hit the gas. The tires screeched against the pavement as the cab sped away into the night.

Behind them, the cab driver sat up on the curb, disoriented, brushing dust from his shirt.

"Asshole!" he shouted after them, shaking a fist.

Then he staggered to his feet and stumbled down the street, still stunned and cursing under his breath.

# CHAPTER 31

Inside the brightly lit emergency room of Northwestern Hospital, the technician wheeled Mary through the automatic double doors at a brisk pace. Lindsey walked tightly beside the gurney, keeping hold of Mary's hand, her face a mask of worry.

A nurse, clad in scrubs and a hurried expression, intercepted them. Lindsey wasted no time.

"She's bleeding!" she shouted, her voice cracking with urgency.

The nurse gave Mary a quick once-over, then nodded to the technician. "Put her in room five."

She turned to Mary, speaking in a calm but clinical voice. "Dr. Richards is on his way. In the meantime, the staff doctor will come and examine you."

Mary's voice broke with panic. "Why am I bleeding? What's wrong?!"

"Ma'am, I can't answer your questions just yet," the nurse replied. "The doctor will be with you shortly. Try to relax."

Relax. The word was meaningless at this moment, but the nurse didn't linger to soothe her further. She turned away, leaving the technician to wheel Mary into the designated exam room.

Once inside, another nurse appeared and helped the technician ease Mary onto the hospital bed. Mary groaned, sweat beading on her brow as she clutched at the thin sheet covering her.

Lindsey hovered beside the bed. "Is the doctor coming soon? She's losing a lot of blood—does he know that?"

The second nurse gave a tired smile, attempting professionalism under pressure. "The doctor is aware. And for the record, the doctor on staff is a woman, and yes she knows."

As if on cue, the door swung open and in walked Dr. Wells—a tall, slender brunette who looked so young she might've still been on her way to prom rather than medical rounds. Her ponytail bounced as she entered confidently, but Mary and Lindsey exchanged doubtful glances. Then Mary screamed, doubling over in pain.

"This is bullshit," Lindsey blurted. "You can't be the doctor."

Dr. Wells didn't flinch. "I can assure you, I am well-qualified. Actually, I'm one of the best obstetricians in the state of Illinois."

She moved to Mary's side and began a thorough examination. Her brows furrowed as she evaluated what she found.

"And I have signed papers that certify that fact," she added.

Mary cried out again, her body writhing on the bed.

Dr. Wells turned to the second nurse. "Prep her for the ultrasound."

"Certainly, doctor."

Dr. Wells walked around to the head of the bed and lowered her voice.

"It appears that you have placenta previa. The ultrasound will confirm the diagnosis and tell us how your baby's doing."

She placed a reassuring hand on Mary's arm and offered the first soft smile of the evening. "Relax. I got you."

With that, the doctor turned and walked out of the room. Lindsey stood for a moment, her head tilting to the side, watching Dr. Wells exit with new—if reluctant—respect.

Mary noticed the change. For once, Lindsey didn't have something sarcastic or cynical to add. No quip. No sigh. Just a subtle shift in posture, like something had impressed her despite herself.

Mary lay back against the pillow, the crinkling of the hospital sheet loud in the otherwise quiet room. The hum of fluorescent lights above and the soft beep of a monitor nearby did little to settle the swirl of thoughts pounding behind her eyes.

**Placenta previa.**

The words echoed, clinical and weighty. They hadn't meant much at first—not until she'd seen the flicker of seriousness in Dr. Wells' eyes. Not until she'd heard the word *ultrasound* paired with *Let's see how your baby's doing*.

That phrasing—it stuck.

Not *how you're doing*.

Not *you'll be fine*.

Just the baby.

Mary's hand instinctively drifted to her abdomen, resting over the hospital gown. She wasn't showing much yet, but she could feel the difference. The faint pressure. The knowledge that someone else was sharing space inside her, asking for protection she wasn't sure she could give.

"Hey," Lindsey said, stepping closer to the bed.

Mary blinked, pulled from her spiraling thoughts. "Yeah?"

"You okay?"

It was such a simple question. But it landed heavier than expected.

Mary offered a small nod, though it wasn't convincing even to herself. "I don't know," she admitted after a beat. "I thought everything was fine. I mean, I didn't think it was supposed to get scary this early."

Lindsey pulled up the plastic chair beside the bed and sat, crossing one leg over the other. "It's always scary," she said. "We just pretend it's not because no one wants to talk about what can go wrong."

The honesty caught Mary off-guard. Not dressed up in sarcasm. Not deflective.

She let out a shaky breath. "I didn't even tell Brad I was coming in."

Lindsey's mouth pulled into a familiar, unimpressed line. "He should've been here anyway."

"I didn't want to bother him."

"You're in a hospital, Mary. That's literally the definition of *bother-worthy*."

Mary gave a half-smile, then glanced toward the doorway Dr. Wells had walked through, wondering how long the test would take. "Do you think she's right? That it's manageable?"

"Stop worrying. She knows what she's doing." Lindsey paused. "And she looked at you like you were worth saving. Not every doctor does that. Trust me."

That landed unexpectedly hard.

Mary swallowed against the lump forming in her throat. Her fingers curled over her stomach again, more protective now. "If something happens to the baby, I don't think I can go through this again."

Lindsey didn't answer right away. She leaned forward, resting her elbows on her knees. "You're not going to have to. But if you do, you'll survive it. You're a lot tougher than you think."

"Am I?" Mary whispered.

Lindsey looked her straight in the eye. "Yeah. You are."

The door creaked open, and a nurse peeked in, clipboard in hand. "Ultrasound tech is on the way. Shouldn't be long."

Mary nodded. The nurse disappeared.

As the door swung shut, the room quieted again.

"Do you think Brad even wants this baby?" Mary asked.

Lindsey's answer was swift. "I think Brad doesn't even know what Brad wants. But that doesn't mean the baby shouldn't be born."

"It will be born, it's just..." Mary paused, as if processing both the answer and the echo of her own fear.

The weight of the moment settled around them, not heavy enough to crush, but enough to reshape the air. Mary reached again for her water cup and sipped her hand steadier this time.

Then she leaned her head back against the pillow, eyes fixed on the ceiling tiles and waited.

# CHAPTER 32

Logan eased the cab into a parking spot and let the engine idle. He reached into his back pocket and pulled out his worn leather wallet. Flipping open the small pad tucked inside, he turned to a blank page and scribbled an address. Without a word, he tore the paper free and handed it to Brad.

"Here's my address," he said. "At least for the next month. Then I'm off to Geneva. I'll send you the new address when I move there." His voice dipped, a flicker of hope sneaking in. "Send me a picture of my grandson. Maybe someday... you'll let me see him."

Brad took the slip of paper and slid it into his wallet without looking at it.

"You helped us," Brad said. "I'll send you a picture. But that's it. That's all there's gonna be between you and my family."

Logan gave a slight nod. He shifted the car into drive and pulled out, heading toward Interstate 215 East.

They drove in silence for a few miles before Dave spoke, his voice low but firm.

"Man, just let it go," he said. "I wish I had a father to forgive. Life's short. We all screw up sometimes."

Brad didn't respond. His fingers flexed against his thigh as he stared ahead.

Dave turned toward him. "Hey—you're wrong, and I gotta call you out. My dad was a complete disaster. Full of flaws. Unbelievable ones. But he was still my dad... and I forgave him."

He paused, voice tightening with something between sorrow and conviction. "I'd give anything to talk to him one more time."

Brad turned to glance at him, but Dave wasn't done.

"You're being a hypocrite."

"What the hell are you talking about?" Brad asked, caught off guard.

"You left your son too."

Brad blinked, taken aback. "What—?"

"Why are you seeing a therapist, huh? Because you don't want to be a father. You're afraid of screwing it up. But in a way... haven't you already left?"

"That makes no sense!" Brad snapped.

Dave met his eyes. "You know it's the truth."

From the front seat, Logan's voice cut in. "You don't want to be a father... because of me?"

Brad didn't answer right away. His jaw clenched. He said, "What do I know about being a father? I haven't got a clue." He looked at Logan. "I had no role model."

Logan gave a bitter smile. "It starts with being there."

Brad scoffed. "How would you know?"

"Because I wasn't there," Logan admitted. "I have money. Lots of it. But family?" He shook his head. "You can't buy that."

Brad glanced at his father for a moment, then looked away, his expression unreadable.

Dave cleared his throat. "Damn, I'm glad Lindsey's not pregnant," he muttered. "I'm leaving her ass. Hello, freedom."

Brad laughed unexpectedly, the tension easing for a second. "Who you kidding? You're not going anywhere."

Dave didn't answer. He turned toward the window, eyes distant, lost in thought.

---

Interstate 215 East crawled with traffic, a glittering line of brake lights snaking ahead into the Vegas dusk. Frustrated travelers blared their horns as cars stood bumper to bumper.

Inside the cabin, the tension thickened.

Logan kept his eyes on the road, both hands resting on the wheel.

"What time's the flight?" he asked.

"Eleven," Brad replied, glancing at his watch.

Dave leaned forward, scanning the standstill ahead. "We'll never make it if this traffic doesn't let up."

"No worries," Logan said, though his eyes flicked to the rearview mirror.

Three cars behind them, a black van with tinted windows kept pace. It had been trailing them since they merged onto the expressway. Logan didn't like it. *Was another shooter in the alley, watching and waiting?*

Up ahead, they crawled past the scene of a wreck—shattered glass, a crumpled sedan, the flashing lights of patrol cars. Once past the scene, the traffic thinned, and movement returned.

"We should make it now," Brad said, letting out a breath.

Logan accelerated, weaving into the next lane. The black van did the same.

Dave, lost in thought, stared out the rain-speckled window. "My wife's cheating on me," he said. "She thinks I don't know."

Logan didn't even blink. "You want me to kill her for you?"

Brad shot him a stern look.

Logan shrugged. "It's what I do."

Brad turned back to Dave. "Is it someone you know?"

Dave shook his head. "No. Some young stud. I got suspicious of all those 'on my own' nights, so I had her followed. I have pictures."

"Damn," Brad muttered. "That's hard."

Dave's voice dropped as he kept his eyes on the passing scenery. "I always knew it was one-sided. But I stayed anyway."

"Life's too short to be with a woman like that," Brad said. "You've got options."

Logan checked the rearview again. The black van was still there. Same distance. Same slow pursuit. His jaw clenched.

They approached the airport exit.

Logan signaled and took it.

So did the van.

As they pulled into the airport parking lot, Brad spoke up. "You don't need to park—just drive us up to the front."

"No," Logan said. "I want to see you off."

Brad glanced at him, eyebrows raised but said nothing.

Logan pulled into a spot near the terminal. The van hadn't turned in yet—but Logan's eyes lingered on the entrance behind them as he shifted the cab into park.

———◦———

The heat outside clung to their backs as Logan, Brad, and Dave stepped out of the stolen cab into the sprawling chaos of the Harry Reid International Airport parking lot. Logan carried the briefcase tightly in one hand, his eyes scanning the horizon. The black van had vanished—nowhere in sight among the rows of cars glinting beneath the overhead lights. Still, Logan stayed tense. Disappearances like that never meant anything good.

They crossed into the airport, swallowed by the rush of travelers hurrying to flights, families reuniting, businesspeople wheeling briefcases, and children tugging on their parents' arms. The aromatic smell of coffee hung in the air along with body odor. But no one gave the loud, bright, and disorienting atmosphere much thought.

At the counter, Brad stepped forward, Dave right beside him, Logan trailing just behind.

"May I help you?" the airport clerk asked with a rehearsed smile.

"Brad Morgan. I reserved online," Brad said.

"One moment." The clerk tapped on the keyboard, then printed the boarding passes. "That will be Gate 14. Take a first left down the hall."

"Thanks," Brad replied, taking the tickets and handing Dave his copy.

They began walking toward the gate.

"I won't force a relationship," Logan said, his voice quieter now, more cautious. "But if you ever want to talk about... well, anything... I—"

GUNSHOTS tore through the air. Panic erupted.

Screams sliced through the terminal. People dove to the floor or fled in every direction. The sharp echo of the shots bounced off the walls. Logan collapsed to the cold tile with a sickening thud, blood exploding from a gaping hole in his skull. His body jerked once, then lay still.

"Logan!" Brad shouted, diving for cover with Dave. They crawled across the floor, pushing past toppled luggage and stampeding feet, until they reached him.

Dave turned and shouted, "Call an ambulance! He's been shot!"

He glanced down. "They took the briefcase," he said grimly.

Brad didn't even respond. He stripped off his shirt and rolled it into a bundle, pressing it beneath Logan's head. Blood poured freely, saturating the fabric, spilling across the floor in bright crimson rivulets.

Logan's breaths were shallow and broken. His eyes fluttered, his body still fighting.

Brad gripped his hand tightly, heart pounding. "Stay with me," he whispered. "Just stay with me."

# CHAPTER 33

The ultrasound machine hummed with quiet urgency as Dr. Wells guided the transducer over Mary's distended abdomen. The room was sterile and bright, but the tension inside made the air thick and hard to breathe. Lindsey stood nearby, observing how Mary's hands trembled as they gripped the thin bed sheets.

Dr. Wells narrowed her eyes at the monitor, her jaw tightening. Mary's gaze bounced between the doctor's expression and the black-and-white flickering screen.

"What is it?" Mary asked, voice strained with panic. "What do you see?"

Dr. Wells turned toward the nurse without answering. Her voice sharpened with command. "Prep her and set up an emergency C-section. Stat."

Mary's body tensed as another wave of pain seized her. She screamed, clutching her belly, her legs trembling as the contractions hit harder and closer.

"What's happening?" she cried. "Where's my doctor? Where is Dr. Richards?"

Dr. Wells faced her, calm but firm. "We don't have time to wait on Dr. Richards. Placenta previa is causing the bleeding."

Mary's eyes widened with terror. "What?"

"When was your last ultrasound with Dr. Richards?" Dr. Wells asked.

"I-I missed the last appointment," Mary admitted, her voice breaking as she turned hysterical. "I didn't think—"

"Listen," Dr. Wells said, her tone softening just a fraction. "I need you to calm down. The baby's heartbeat is normal for now, but to avoid any complications, I'm recommending a C-section immediately."

"No!" Mary gasped, shaking her head. "No C-section! I want a normal... a vaginal birth. I planned for it. I wrote it down—I want it."

Dr. Wells' face darkened with the weight of responsibility. "There can be serious complications."

Another contraction hit, brutal and fast. Mary let out another anguished scream.

"You said you were the best!" she shouted, half-pleading, half-accusing.

Dr. Wells gave a tight, almost sympathetic smile. "I am the best."

She leaned in closer, her voice low and grave, each word weighed with urgency. "But I am not irresponsible. You will have a C-section, or you can wait here for another doctor to watch you, and your baby die in this room."

Lindsey stepped forward, aghast. "What a bitch!"

Dr. Wells didn't even blink. Her eyes locked on Mary's. "What's it going to be, Mary? Are you going to let me do my job? Or do I really have to become the bitch your friend thinks I am?"

Mary's face crumpled as she dropped her head into her hands. Her body shook with sobs.

"Doctor..." she whispered, her voice cracking, barely audible. "Please... save my son."

Dr. Wells gave a single nod. Without another word, she turned and exited the room, her posture taut with focus and resolve. Lindsey stood beside Mary in stunned silence, the weight of the moment anchoring them both.

The echo of Mary's whispered plea—*Please... save my son*—still hovered in the air like smoke that refused to clear. Lindsey had never heard her friend sound so hollow, so stripped of strength. It wasn't just fear. It was surrender.

Mary's shoulders shook beneath the thin hospital gown, her face buried in her hands, as if curling into herself could stop the world from falling apart.

Lindsey didn't know what to do. She was used to giving advice, not comfort. Jabs, not gentleness. She reached out awkwardly, laying a hand on Mary's back. The sobs deepened, full-bodied and raw, like something primal had broken loose.

Lindsey looked toward the door Dr. Wells had just walked through. The woman had left like a force of nature—precise, unsentimental, absolute. Lindsey had called her a bitch under her breath more than once tonight. But now, that word felt juvenile. Petty. It was a name people used when they didn't understand authority wrapped in urgency.

She understood it now.

She glanced back down at Mary, still crumpled in the hospital bed.

"Hey," Lindsey said, crouching beside her. "I'm here, okay? I'm not going anywhere."

Mary didn't answer. Her fingers tightened around her face, as if shielding herself from a blow that had already landed. Her body rocked with sobs, but she no longer made a sound.

Lindsey reached for her hand, coaxing it away from her face. "You did the right thing," she said. "You asked her to fight. And I think... I think she will."

Mary's tear-swollen eyes met hers, and for the first time, Lindsey saw something more than fear—she saw a quiet, flickering grief. A mother's awareness that she might lose her baby before ever hearing his cry.

"I didn't want to be here without Brad," Mary whispered. "He should've been here."

Lindsey nodded. "He should've. But he's not. I'm all you've got."

Mary gave a faint, broken nod and squeezed Lindsey's hand like it was the only thing tethering her to this side of hope.

A nurse entered a moment later, her tone gentle but direct. "We're going to prep her for the OR. You can stay until they take her down."

Lindsey stood, giving Mary's hand one last squeeze before stepping aside. The nurse began unfastening monitors, checking vitals, adjusting IV bags with swift, practiced movements. It all looked so methodical—like none of it could possibly hold the weight of what was happening.

Lindsey backed into the corner of the room and just watched. Her chest ached, though she couldn't tell if it was from guilt or fear. Maybe all of it. She'd come tonight thinking Mary needed moral support—a ride, a pep talk, maybe a shoulder to cry on.

She hadn't expected this. Blood. Surgery. Her friend on the edge of life and loss.

A part of her wanted to leave the room before the gurney arrived. She wasn't good with hospitals. She wasn't good with this kind of pain. But she stayed.

Because Mary was still holding on. And so was she.

# CHAPTER 34

The echo of the gunshots still reverberated in Brad's ears, dulled by the blinding grief that surged forward as he knelt beside his father. Logan lay sprawled on the airport floor, blood soaking into Brad's shirt beneath his head. The noise of the panicked terminal blurred into a distant hum as Brad gripped his father's hand.

"Don't talk," Brad murmured, trying to steady his voice. "Save your strength."

But Logan's hand twitched, patting weakly at his pants pocket.

"I... my... keys," he gasped, his voice a rasp. "Take my... keys... special door... special door..."

His breath was shallow, erratic.

Dave leaned in. "He's trying to tell you something."

"Yeah," Brad muttered, eyes fixed on Logan's paling face. "But what?"

He looked down as Logan's trembling fingers reached for Brad's hand and pressed it toward the pocket of his pants. Brad understood. He reached inside and pulled out the keys, the metal cold and slick with blood. He leaned in close, listening as his father tried to speak.

"My house... keys... door..." Logan managed, blinking, his focus fading.

Brad's grip tightened around the keys. His father was slipping away. "Just hold on," he said, his voice cracking. "Help is coming."

But Logan's body was failing. His breath grew more labored. His lips moved again, barely forming the words.

"I'm... sorry... Forgive me, I—"

Brad didn't wait. He leaned down, close enough to feel his father's dying breath on his cheek.

"I forgive you," Brad whispered. "And I... I love you. You can go now."

A long, deep exhale left Logan's chest. Brad felt the weight of it. An acknowledgment. A release. Then nothing.

Logan's eyes stilled, wide open and glassy. Brad reached out and lowered his father's eyelids with trembling fingers.

Dave stood nearby, saying nothing. There was nothing to say. The briefcase was gone. Blood pooled on the tiles. People still screamed in the distance. But in that moment, Brad knelt over his father's body, his shoulders heaving, as the pain cracked through him and the tears came without mercy.

The sound of them startled even him. Guttural. Wet. Deep from somewhere he didn't know still existed. It was a sob that didn't care who heard it—didn't ask for privacy or dignity. It just tore loose from his chest like something primal and broken.

Logan Mulroney—killer, liar, mystery—lay still beneath him. Not just still. Gone.

The same man who'd haunted Brad's childhood like a ghost now lay before him like a warning—bloodied, emptied, finished.

And despite everything Logan had done—or hadn't done—Brad had said the words anyway.

*I forgive you.*

Maybe it was true. Maybe it was just the heat of the moment. But something inside him had needed to say it. For Logan. For himself.

His fingers hovered over Logan's chest, wanting to feel another breath, hoping for a twitch, a flicker—anything to prove the moment hadn't passed.

But the silence spoke volumes.

No heartbeat. No movement.

Just the metallic tang of blood in the air and the cold draft of a door swinging open somewhere far down the corridor.

Dave stood behind him, unmoving, arms crossed tight across his chest. Brad couldn't read his face—shock, maybe. Restraint. Or maybe he was just letting Brad have the moment untouched.

The pain came again, this time quieter, more insidious. The kind that didn't scream, but clung—wrapping around his ribs and lungs, making it hard to breathe.

"I didn't think it would feel like this," Brad muttered.

Dave didn't respond.

Brad wiped his face with the sleeve of his jacket, but it did nothing. The tears just kept coming. "I thought I'd be angry. Or relieved. But this..."

He looked down at Logan's face again. It looked softer now. Younger. Like the rage and calculation had drained out and left only bone, blood, and skin.

"I spent most of my life hating him," Brad said. "And he still died holding the one thing I never really gave him."

Dave took a step closer, crouched down beside him. "You gave him what mattered."

Brad shook his head. "Too late."

Dave placed a hand on his shoulder. "Sometimes... it's enough that it got said at all."

In the distance, sirens were growing louder. Someone called them. It isn't over yet. Not by a long shot.

But this part—this chapter—had closed.

Brad looked at the blood pooling around Logan's coat, spreading toward the edge of the tiles. *Was the briefcase worth it?*

He glanced back up at Dave. "In the end, he tried."

"Yeah," Dave said. "He did."

The weight of it all—the debts, the lies, the legacy of violence—settled on Brad's back like wet cement. But he didn't move. He let himself kneel there a moment longer, grounding himself in the pain. Not to wallow—but to feel it. All of it. The kind of grief that resets a man. Or breaks him.

"I have to leave him here," Brad said. "Don't I?"

Dave nodded. "Yeah. The ambulance will be here, there's nothing more you can do."

Brad looked down one last time, placed his palm over Logan's now-still chest, and whispered a final thank-you—not because he was sure he meant it, but because it felt right.

Then he stood.

The world came rushing back all at once—shouting, sirens, running footsteps.

# CHAPTER 35

Mary lay on the operating table, sedated but still conscious, her face pale beneath the harsh brilliance of Gardnerville Memorial Hospital's surgical lights. Her breathing was shallow, her gaze unfocused, pupils sluggish under the influence of mild anesthesia. Beeping monitors tracked her vital signs in soft, rhythmic pulses, like a mechanical lullaby barely masking the stakes beneath.

Dr. Wells hovered over her, flanked by two nurses and a technician, her gloved hands moving with the precise urgency of someone who had done this a hundred times but knew that didn't guarantee success.

Behind the thick glass of the observation window, Lindsey stood in borrowed surgical scrubs, arms crossed tightly over her chest. She wasn't supposed to be here—observers weren't encouraged during active procedures—but she had begged, pleaded, until someone allowed her to watch from the hallway. Even here, her presence was tolerated, not welcomed.

She leaned closer to the glass, fogging it with her breath. "You will feel some pressure, but no pain," Dr. Wells said inside the room, her voice muffled through the barrier but still audible.

"I think she might actually know what she's doing," Lindsey whispered under her breath, a half-smile tugging at her lips. The words weren't for anyone else. Just a threadbare attempt to ground herself.

Inside, Mary managed a faint smile—just a twitch at the corners of her mouth—as if some part of her could still feel Lindsey nearby.

Then it happened. A sudden, shrill alarm split the air.

Red lights flashed on the monitors. One of the nurses rushed to the side panel, adjusting settings. The calm, sterile rhythm fractured in an instant.

"She's hemorrhaging! Fetal distress!" Dr. Wells barked, her calm unraveling as she snapped into action.

Lindsey's body slammed upright. Her heart thudded so hard she could feel it in her throat. "No, no, no—" she whispered. Her palms flattened against the glass, helpless.

Mary's eyes widened in a burst of panic. "No! No!" she gasped, her voice ragged with fear.

But there was no time. Dr. Wells had already reached for a syringe, her movements swift and clinical. "You'll be okay," she murmured, plunging the needle into Mary's arm. "We've got you."

Mary's frame softened as the drug spread through her bloodstream. Her eyelids fluttered. Her limbs slackened. Just like that, she was slipping under—whether from sedation or something far worse, Lindsey couldn't tell.

The nurse closest to the window glanced up and caught sight of Lindsey. She stepped away from the commotion just long enough to approach the glass, her expression tight but composed. She didn't open the door—just held up a hand and mouthed the words.

*"We've got her."*

It wasn't rude. It wasn't dismissive.

It was the kind of assurance that told you: We're trying. But don't interfere.

Lindsey didn't move at first. Her hands were fists at her sides, white-knuckled and useless. But she nodded.

She gave Mary one last look—her friend, the one who always tried to keep it together for everyone else. But now her body was betraying her in real time, her strength unraveling beneath surgical lights and urgent commands.

She turned from the glass and stepped back into the corridor.

Every step hurts.

Each footfall was heavy, as if gravity itself had thickened around her. The distance between her and that door felt infinite. Her friend—her almost-sister—was inside, and she was out here.

She exited into the main hallway, blinking under the clinical hum of fluorescent lights. The quiet outside the OR felt like a slap. Not peace—absence. The kind of absence that leaves you gasping.

Her footsteps faltered. She turned, her body aching to storm back through those doors, to scream for someone to talk to her, to beg them to do more—*something*. But she'd already seen Dr. Wells' expression through the glass: all sharp lines and hard resolve.

That was not a woman who allowed chaos in her space.

That was a woman preparing for war.

Lindsey backed into a wall and sank onto a cold metal bench beside a vending machine humming with indifference. Her hands were still shaking. She curled them into fists, pressing them against her knees. The faint smell of latex and hospital soap clung to her palms, nauseating now.

She tried to call Dave. Her thumb hovered over the contact.

She hung up before it rang.

Tried Brad. Straight to voicemail.

"Dammit," she muttered, her voice low, broken at the edges.

A code echoed from the intercom—three sharp chimes followed by a rapid sequence of numbers. She held her breath, waiting for confirmation.

Not theirs. Not yet.

She stared down the hallway. A nurse passed, then another. No one made eye contact. No one stopped. Everyone moved with purpose, and Lindsey felt like a smudge on the edge of a painting—something that didn't belong but couldn't be erased.

She looked back toward the operating room doors. They were sealed now, impenetrable, no windows, no whispers from within.

Inside, everything was happening. And she was nothing but a bystander.

"I should've stayed closer," she murmured. "Should've fought harder to be in there."

The thought gnawed at her. She didn't know if Mary could feel her absence—or if it even mattered—but she felt it. And it hurt.

Then, like breath slipping from a body, she whispered, "Come on, Mary... stay."

She didn't know what she meant. Stay alive. Stay strong. Stay with *me*.

But the words were out there now, unanchored. Floating down sterile halls. Drifting through steel doors.

And inside the OR, Mary's life—and the baby's—hung in the balance.

# CHAPTER 36

A cab pulled up to the curb in front of a modest apartment complex. The building was clean but unremarkable, tucked between a laundromat and a shuttered bakery. The cab slowed to a stop, and Brad stepped out first. Dave followed, squinting up at the building with a mix of impatience and curiosity.

Dave leaned back toward the open cab window. "We'll only be a little while. Keep the meter going," he told the driver, who gave a half-hearted nod and leaned back in his seat, already scrolling through his phone.

As the cab idled behind them, Dave caught up to Brad, who was already at the front entrance.

"Why are we here?" Dave asked, frowning. "We should be headed home."

Brad didn't look back. "It'll only take a minute."

Dave let out a sharp breath but followed.

Brad took out the keyring he'd pulled from his father's pocket at the airport. He tried several keys, jiggling one after another in the lock. None of them worked. He muttered under his breath, trying again.

On the fourth attempt, the lock clicked. The door creaked open with a reluctant groan. Brad stepped inside, and Dave followed, glancing around the dark entryway.

The door closed behind them with a solid thud.

---

Snoop padded into the room, his gray fur catching a shaft of sunlight streaming through the blinds. The cat rubbed against Brad's leg, purring loud and steady like a motor. Brad squatted down and ran a hand along the cat's back, scratching behind its ears.

"Hey, buddy," he muttered, more to himself than to the animal.

His gaze drifted across the room to the coffee table. There, as if waiting for him, stood a familiar bottle of Jura Scotch—half-full and glinting amber in the light. Brad stood and walked over. He uncapped it, poured himself a drink into a nearby glass, and took a slow sip. The burn in his throat was soothing.

He turned and held the bottle out to Dave. "You want one?"

Dave waved a hand. "I'll pass. It's barely noon."

Brad shrugged, took another sip, and kept the bottle in hand as he wandered further into the apartment. Dave followed, and Snoop followed them both.

They reached a room that looked more like a study than a bedroom. A sleek black desk sat beneath a wide window, flanked by shelves lined with books, folders, and metal lockboxes. The furniture was expensive, clean, and eerily precise.

"Wow," Dave said, stepping in. "Now this is nice."

Brad glanced around with a cynical smirk. "Yeah. The lifestyle of a highly paid killer."

He dropped into the desk chair and started rummaging through the drawers. Paperclips, maps, blueprints. He pulled out a black leather-bound notebook. He flipped it open, thumbing through pages until his eyes settled on a list near the back.

TO DO BEFORE GENEVA

Pick up new ID

Lease apartment

Dispose of all weapons

Get carriage for Snoop

Send money to Mildred

Celebrate

Brad held the book up for Dave to see. "He was planning to retire—in Geneva!"

Dave didn't respond. He just shook his head his face unreadable.

Brad tossed the notebook to the floor. It landed face-down with a soft thud, as Snoop leapt onto the desk and curled beside the scattered papers, perfectly at home in the quiet chaos his owner had left behind.

Brad rifled through another drawer beneath the desk, but it came up empty. He sighed in frustration.

"We're just wasting our time," he muttered.

Dave stood to leave, but as Brad stepped away from the desk, Snoop let out a sharp, almost human-like squeal. The cat darted across the room and began clawing frantically at the knob of a closed door.

Dave paused. "Didn't he whisper something about a door?"

Brad turned toward the feline, eyes narrowing. "Yeah. He did. Maybe this is it."

He pulled out Logan's keyring and began testing each one in the lock. After a few seconds, a soft click signaled success. Brad pushed the door open.

"Wow," Dave breathed. "He was organized."

Brad stepped into the small, windowless room. The first few drawers he opened were filled with guns—everything from compact pistols to high-powered rifles. Drawer after drawer of arranged weapons, ready to take on anyone at any time.

"Why would he want me to see all these guns?" Brad muttered. "I can't use them. This is bullshit."

He crossed to the opposite wall and opened another drawer. Inside were white dress shirts, neatly folded. He dumped them on the floor. Nothing. The next drawer—nothing again.

Then he opened another.

Rows and rows of neatly bundled one-hundred-dollar bills stared back at him.

"Damn," Brad said, eyes wide. "Look at how much money is here!"

Dave stepped forward. "He stashed all of his hit money here!"

Brad opened another drawer—more money. And another—still more. They shared a stunned look.

Accidentally he brushed against a small button near the edge of the drawer. With a quiet whir, the wall rotated, revealing another wall behind it.

They froze, staring.

The hidden wall was lined with photographs. Dozens of them. Pictures of a young Brad—holding karate trophies, wearing Little League uniforms, tossing a pitch from the mound, standing in cap and gown at his high school graduation, and again at college.

Dave's voice was soft. "Who was this man?"

Brad didn't answer right away. He stepped closer, touched one of the frames, and removed a photo showing Logan with his arms around a young version of himself. Both of them were beaming.

"A stranger," Brad said, his voice tight. "He was my father."

Dave placed a hand on his shoulder. "Hey, man... let's go home."

Brad didn't move. "I have to make a stop first."

While Brad continued to scan the room, Dave wandered into the kitchen and returned with a large garbage bag. He began stuffing it with cash from the drawers.

"What are you looking for?" Dave asked.

"A name," Brad said. "The name of his boss."

Dave frowned. "There's enough money here. Why are you looking for trouble? Does it really matter who he is?"

"It matters," Brad said. "Where's that pad?"

He walked over to where the notepad had landed on the floor and picked it up. Flipping through it, he paused on a particular page.

Scrawled in Logan's handwriting: "SEE PARKER, NEW JOB."

Brad let out a frustrated sigh. "That doesn't help."

But then he noticed the pad was branded. The logo at the top: *The Venetian*.

"Shit," Brad muttered. "Parker could be in the same damn hotel!"

Dave shook his head. "Who the fuck cares?"

Brad ignored him and strode over to the gun cases. He picked up a large-barreled rifle, tested its weight, then set it down. Instead, he grabbed the .357 Magnum revolver. He opened the chamber and loaded it calmly, methodically.

Dave's voice cut through the tense silence. "Man, you have a wife at home who genuinely loves you... who's about to have your baby. Don't throw that away. It's rare."

Brad stood at the front door, the revolver tucked in his waistband. He glanced back.

"You coming?"

Dave hesitated for a beat, then lifted the garbage bag filled with cash onto his shoulder.

Again, he followed.

# CHAPTER 37

The grand interior of the Venetian Hotel shimmered under crystal chandeliers and golden light. Everything glistened—floor tiles polished to a mirror sheen, roulette wheels spinning with hypnotic grace, and poker tables lined with high-rollers and hopefuls, each with their own desperation hidden behind chips and charm. Brad and Dave moved through the labyrinth of tables and ringing slot machines, the clatter of coins and jubilant screams from lucky winners clashing with the quiet storm brewing inside Brad's head.

Brad slowed as they neared a blackjack table. The sleek felt of the surface, the crisp snap of cards, the promise of risk and reward, it all pulled at him. With a thick knot of cash in his pocket and his nerves frayed, the temptation was undeniable. He looked down at the table, then back at Dave.

"Deal me in," Brad said, his voice low, almost detached.

They took seats side by side. The dealer nodded and began to shuffle. The cards flicked across the table with mechanical rhythm, precise and cold. Brad stared at his hand but didn't see it. The world around him blurred.

In his mind, images flashed like lightning bolts tearing across a dark sky.

He saw the foreclosure notice, bold red ink declaring the loss of their home. Hooded shooters bursting through his front door—chaos, violence, fear. His wife's face in a hospital room, pale and broken. Cindy, the woman who had drawn him into this mess, bleeding out in his arms, her eyes dimming as life fled from her. Logan—his father—dying, clutching Brad's hand, asking for forgiveness too late.

Each vision hit like a punch to the chest. He looked down at the cards again. They meant nothing.

With a sharp exhale, Brad pushed his cards away. "Fold," he muttered, rising from the chair.

Dave glanced up, his brow furrowing as Brad stepped back from the table, urgency written all over his face.

"Wait here," Brad said, a new fire kindling in his voice. "I need to do this."

Dave gave him a small nod, leaning back in his chair. "Go handle your business," he said, his tone calm but knowing.

Brad didn't reply. He turned and disappeared into the crowd, the lights of the casino flashing off the sweat on his neck, his fists clenched and his purpose clear.

———◆———

Brad entered the opulent lobby of the Venetian, its marble floors gleaming beneath the chandeliers. The scent of polished wood and expensive perfume filled the air. He walked purposefully toward the front desk, tension threading through every step. Behind the counter, a young hotel clerk glanced up from her screen, smiling with practiced ease.

"How can I help you, Mr. Morgan?" she asked.

Brad leaned in, keeping his voice low but steady. "I'm looking for... Parker. Does he work here?"

The clerk's eyes flickered with recognition, but she didn't miss a beat. "Of course. Thirty-sixth floor, last office on the left."

"Thank you," Brad said.

"Certainly, Mr. Morgan," she replied with a courteous nod.

Brad moved away from the desk and toward the row of elevators at the back of the lobby. He pressed the button, the metal doors sliding open with a chime. As the elevator ascended, Brad adjusted his coat, feeling the weight of the .357 Magnum under his arm. His reflection in the mirrored walls stared back—worn, haunted, determined.

The elevator dinged again, and the doors parted to reveal a long, silent corridor lined with offices. Thick carpet muted his footsteps as he walked to the end of the hall. The last door on the left stood ajar. Brad pushed it open.

Inside, Parker lounged behind an enormous mahogany desk, puffing on one of his signature cigars. The room was dim, smoky, and lined with dark wood paneling. The stench of power and secrecy lingered like old cologne.

"Parker?" Brad asked, stepping fully into the room.

Parker exhaled a plume of smoke and smiled. "We finally meet!"

Brad didn't smile back. "Let me formally introduce myself."

He walked across the office and stopped at the edge of the desk. In one swift motion, he pulled the .357 Magnum from under his coat. A deafening *BANG* shattered the stillness, and Parker howled in pain, blood spurting from where Brad's bullet grazed his ear.

"Damn," Brad muttered. "I guess I need more training."

Parker clutched his ear, eyes wide in disbelief, his fingers slick with blood. He reached beneath his desk, but Brad lunged forward and slammed his arm down, knocking it away from the hidden button.

"It's just you and me," Brad said coldly.

Parker's face contorted in pain and disbelief. "So, I see you have some of your father's shortcomings," he spat. "You should've killed me when you had the chance."

Brad kept the gun raised, unwavering. "I'm a gambler," he said, "but this isn't a gamble. Not this time. When I walk out of this room, you'll be dead."

"You underestimate me," Parker growled, wiping his bloodied hand with a tissue. "Just like your father did."

He paused, composed himself, then leaned back in his chair, cigar still clutched between his fingers.

"I tell you what," Parker said, his tone shifting. "As a favor to your old man, I'll forget this... lapse of judgment. I made your father a rich man. He was an ingrate, but you—" He grinned. "You've got potential. Come work for me. I can make you just as rich. Richer."

Brad's expression didn't change, but something flickered behind his eyes. The tension in his grip eased.

"How rich?" he asked.

Parker's grin widened. "Cess-pool rich."

Brad let out a low chuckle. "That's pretty damn rich." He tilted his head, weighing the offer. Then his smile disappeared. "But, you know, I think I'll pass."

Parker's eyes narrowed. "I see you survived the bomb pretty well. So, what do you want? I have my money. We're square."

Brad stepped closer, his voice now colder than before. "No... we'll never be square. You killed my father."

Parker took a slow drag from his cigar, letting the smoke roll from his nostrils as he studied Brad like a chess opponent across the board.

"And now you want to train me to kill?" Brad asked, plain disgust in his tone.

Parker's chuckle came like gravel. "Damn... it's probably in your genes."

The tension in the room surged to a fever pitch. Brad raised the .357 Magnum, the cold steel steady in his hand as he leveled it at Parker's smug, cigar-smeared face. His finger curled around the trigger, but before he could fire, the door behind him BURST open with a crack of splintering wood. Heavy boots pounded against the tile. He barely turned before being blindsided by the rush—Parker's men flooded in like a black wave.

The impact caught Brad off guard. He lost his footing, and the revolver slipped from his grip, clattering to the marble floor.

Parker stood behind his desk with that same infuriating calm, grinding the stub of his cigar into the ashtray with a slow, deliberate twist.

"My men keep me under surveillance all the time," he said coldly, "just so scumbags like you can't get to me."

The stink of ash and sweat filled the air.

"Unfortunately for you," Parker continued, stepping out from behind the desk with a glint of sadistic delight in his eyes, "the job is off the table—and so is your incredibly stupid life."

He gave a small wave of his hand, a king flicking a pawn off the board. "Take him away."

Two of the goons lunged. One grabbed Brad by the arm. THUD! Brad twisted and delivered a vicious front elbow to the first man's skull. The sound of cracking bone echoed as the man crumpled unconscious to the floor.

The second goon pulled a gun.

Brad pivoted, planted his foot, and unleashed a swift, precise roundhouse kick. His heel smashed into the goon's wrist. GUN-SHOT! The weapon discharged wildly, the bullet catching the man in his own leg. He screamed and dropped the gun.

A third thug grabbed Brad from behind, locking his arms. Before he could tighten the hold, Brad slipped his body downward and shifted, breaking free with a forearm block. But the fourth goon was already on him, fists flying. One punch, two, three—pummeling Brad in the ribs and jaw. Blood slicked Brad's lower lip. He spit crimson onto the floor.

The fourth man reached for his gun.

"Let's end this," he snarled.

He cocked the weapon.

Brad's eyes flared with adrenaline. With a sharp pivot, he dropped low and sprang backward, driving his foot into the thug's midsection. The man gasped as the kick knocked the wind out of him, sending him crashing against the wall. The gun clattered to the floor and skidded away.

Brad dove, grabbing the fallen pistol. Then, like a man reclaiming something sacred, he swept over to where he'd dropped the .357 Magnum. He picked it up, both weapons in hand.

His gaze flicked between them.

"I'd much rather kill you with my father's gun," Brad muttered.

He dropped the other firearm with a metallic thunk and turned to face Parker.

Panic replaced bravado in Parker's eyes.

"In minutes, more men will be here," Parker warned, his voice thin, cracking.

"I know," Brad said. "But they can't help you."

The Magnum clicked ominously as Brad cocked it. Parker raised both trembling hands in surrender.

"Killing me makes you just like your father," Parker said, trying to dig deep for one last play.

Brad's hands trembled. The weight of the gun, the ghosts of everything that had come before—it pressed on his chest like a tombstone.

"You're right," Brad whispered.

He lowered the Magnum.

"It would make me just like him. A cold-blooded killer."

He turned, his footsteps echoing through the silence, and walked out the door.

Down the hall.

Five steps. Ten.

He stopped.

The air hung heavily behind him, still thick with the stench of smoke and blood.

With his fingers clenched, he turned back.

He walked again, slower now. Deliberate. He re-entered the office. Parker sat hunched, wide-eyed, bleeding at the ear, disbelief frozen on his face.

Brad didn't hesitate. He lifted the .357 Magnum and, in one smooth motion, pulled the trigger three times.

PFT. PFT. PFT.

The silencer reduced each shot to a dull whisper. But the damage was loud and final. Parker's body slumped over the desk, a trail of blood arcing across the polished surface. Then he slipped off the edge and collapsed onto the floor.

Brad stepped forward, crouched near the lifeless face.

He whispered, "That's for my father. And when you see him... and you will... tell him we're square."

Then he rose, turned, and sprinted out of the room, his footsteps fading into the corridor as sirens began to wail somewhere far below.

━━━━◆○◆━━━━

Brad emerged from the elevator with fire still burning in his chest and blood pounding in his ears. The weight of the .357 Magnum was gone now—wiped clean and discarded in a stairwell trash can two floors up—but the burden of what he'd just done still clung to his shoulders like a second skin.

He moved through the gleaming halls of the Venetian, weaving past tourists, poker junkies, and bachelorette parties, until he spotted Dave in the same spot he'd left him—slouched in a chair near the blackjack tables, pretending not to be bored out of his mind. Dave saw Brad's approach and immediately stood up, catching the urgency in his friend's expression.

"We have to get out of here," Brad said under his breath, eyes scanning the casino like a hunted man.

Dave didn't ask questions. He just nodded.

Without another word, the two men slipped on their sunglasses in unison. A silent ritual. A quiet farewell to subtlety. Whatever had just happened upstairs, Dave didn't need to know—not yet. What mattered was that they leave and leave now.

They moved as one through the golden-lit corridors, past glittering slot machines and gaudy velvet drapes. Dave's limp slowed them, but not enough to matter. Brad's stride was easy, but there was a menace behind the calm. Together, they looked like two gangsters walking away from a job well done—or a city left burning behind them.

One strolled. The other limped. But neither of them looked back.

# CHAPTER 38

The bedroom was cloaked in quiet sunlight, the mid-afternoon rays slanting through the blinds like thin bars of gold. Dave limped from the walk-in closet to the bed, his jaw tight, his movements tense but determined. A dull throb pulsed in his leg with every step, but he ignored it. His focus was singular—packing. Two suitcases lay open on the bed like gaping mouths, half-filled with clothes, shoes, and personal things that no longer belonged to this house.

He yanked a shirt from a hanger and tossed it into the suitcase, then reached for a pair of jeans. The movement made him wince, but he didn't stop. He was done stopping. He was done waiting.

The bedroom door creaked open. Lindsey stood in the threshold, her expression uncertain.

"Did you just get back?" she asked, her voice neutral.

"Yeah," Dave said without looking up. "Just now."

He kept packing, ignoring the silence between them. Lindsey took a step closer, her eyes narrowing as she noticed his limp.

"What's wrong with your leg?"

He didn't respond. His hands moved faster, almost frantically now, as if the act of stuffing things into a suitcase might block out the questions.

"What are you doing?" she asked.

Dave zipped one of the suitcases with force and looked up, his voice hard. "I'm moving on with my life."

Her eyes flicked to the packed bags, then back to his face. Panic crept into her tone. "Can't we talk about this?"

He snapped upright and turned to face her fully. The pain in his leg was nothing compared to the heat boiling in his chest.

"Oh, now you want to talk?" he snapped. "What is it? What do you want to say? I can't hear you!"

Lindsey flinched at the sharpness in his voice.

"This is just so sudden," she stammered. "We don't have to do this right now."

She reached for his arm, desperate to bridge the distance. But Dave pulled away, shrugging her off like a memory he no longer needed.

"I've already left the building," he said bitterly. "You're on your own tonight."

With one last tug, he closed the suitcase like he was sealing off a chapter he never wanted to write. He straightened, adjusting the brim of his cherished Panama Montecristi fedora—less style now, more armor—and wrapped his fingers around the handles as if they might steady him.

He didn't speak. Just limped past her, each step uneven but deliberate, the silence between them louder than any goodbye. Lindsey couldn't move, couldn't breathe. Her lips hung open, trembling, as the front door shut behind him with the soft, brutal weight of something breaking—for good.

Lindsey didn't move.

She stood frozen in the center of the room, her hand still hovering in midair where it had reached for him, fingers curled in empty space. Her chest rose and fell in small, shallow bursts, as if breathing had become too complicated a task.

The silence that followed Dave's exit was not peaceful. It was jagged. Raw. The kind that hummed in the walls and screamed through the floorboards.

He'd left.

Not in anger. Not in haste.

He had left like a man who meant it.

Her eyes traced the room without seeing it—the coffee cup he never finished, the couch pillow still indented from where he'd sat, the crooked frame above the fireplace that she'd always meant to fix. Ordinary things that now felt like evidence from a life that no longer existed.

She turned in a slow, stunned circle, as if trying to rewind time by physically moving backward.

But the suitcase was gone.

And so was he.

Her knees buckled. She was falling. She sank to the floor with a soft thud, the carpet catching her like a witness to collapse. Her hands pressed into the fibers, fists tightening as the reality pushed through her ribcage and settled like stone.

Dave.

He was the one who used to crack dumb jokes in the car when she cried. The one who memorized her coffee order without asking. The one who would pull her into bed at night like he was afraid she'd disappear before morning.

And now he had vanished.

Not all at once. But in pieces. Over months. Over silences. Over every night she rolled away from him and told herself tomorrow would be better.

*You're on your own tonight.*

The words came back sharp and cold. Not just a warning. A sentence.

Her eyes burned, but no tears came. It was worse than crying. It was the stillness before the scream.

She crawled toward the chair he'd been sitting in, reached out with trembling fingers, and touched the armrest as if it could bring him back.

There was nothing left there but warmth.

His scent—cologne, salt, something human—lingered in the room. She hated how it comforted her. Hated how badly she wanted to open the door and call after him. But she didn't move. Couldn't.

Because if she called, and he didn't come back...

That would be worse than this.

She rested her forehead against the side of the chair, jaw clenched. "You left before, Dave," she whispered. "But you always came back."

This time, he hadn't looked back.

He hadn't looked at all, and in her heart, she knew.

He wouldn't be back.

A wind picked up outside, rattling the porch light. *He might lose his hat.* The fedora had always looked ridiculous to her when he first bought it. Too big, too serious. Now, she could still see it in her mind as he adjusted it—less fashion, more armor against the wind. He wore it like a man stepping into battle.

Only the battle had been her. And tonight, he'd surrendered.

No. Not surrendered. He'd chosen to retreat. Permanently.

The house felt cavernous now. Too many walls. Too few reasons to stay.

Lindsey stood legs numb, body hollowed. She walked to the door, pressed her hand against the cool wood, and leaned in—not to open it, but to feel something. Anything.

It was just a door.

But it had become a tombstone.

And Dave, the man who once promised forever, was now just another ghost in the house.

# CHAPTER 39

The lobby of Joliet Bank & Trust gleamed with polished marble and quiet professionalism, but heads still turned as Brad Morgan walked in like he owned the place. Gone were the worn jeans and anxious eyes of a man barely holding it together. Today, he was a different breed—tailored Armani suit clinging to his frame like a second skin, gold cufflinks gleaming subtly beneath a crisp white shirt. His stride was confident, unhurried. He didn't just walk—he *strolled*.

The same bank teller who had once looked through him like a ghost now lifted her head as he approached. Her brows rose in instant recognition.

"Mr. Morgan," she said, her voice warm with surprise and a touch of respect that hadn't been there before.

Brad offered her a slight smile, charismatic and assured. "I need a cashier's check for three hundred thousand," he said.

The words hung in the air like a dropped crystal.

They didn't shatter. They were just suspended there in the air, fragile, shining, impossible to ignore.

The teller blinked. "Ah... did you mean three thousand?" she asked, her fingers hovering above the keyboard, unsure whether to laugh, correct him, or alert security.

Brad shook his head, the smile never leaving his face. It wasn't the kind of smile he wore when he was trying to charm his way out of overdraft fees or talk his way into a week's grace. No—this one was new. Sharp. Intentional. Almost rehearsed.

"No," he said clearly. "Three hundred thousand."

She paused.

The clatter of keyboards around them faded to a muffled rhythm. Somewhere nearby, a printer hummed. The scent of artificial lemon cleaner wafted in from the lobby. But everything slowed inside that small glass window, like the moment had its own gravity.

Then she typed.

Her fingers moved delicately, like she didn't trust the number he'd given her to be real.

But when the screen lit up and revealed his balance, her entire demeanor shifted.

Her eyebrows twitched upward. The corners of her mouth lifted. And then—professionalism kicked in like muscle memory. Her posture straightened, her shoulders squared. She wasn't talking to a deadbeat anymore. She was talking to someone who mattered.

"Well then... how has your day been going, Mr. Morgan?" she asked, the question coated in freshly discovered admiration.

Brad glanced down at his Rolex—new, flawless, ticking with authority—and then back up at her.

"My day couldn't be brighter," he said, voice smooth, polished.

She nodded reverently and stood, walking briskly to the back counter. She returned with the cashier's check held in both hands, like it might melt if not handled properly. The paper had weight.

Ink that bled authority. His name printed with a kind of gravity he hadn't felt in years.

"Is there anything else I could—?"

"No," Brad said smoothly, already turning away. "That'll do."

And just like that, he strolled out of the bank like a man untouched by the world he used to beg from.

His shoes clicked across the marble floor. Not rushed. Not timid. Measured. Confident. Heads didn't turn—but eyes did. Just enough. The security guard by the door gave him a slight nod. The receptionist smiled too long as he passed.

Brad pushed through the glass exit and stepped into the sunlight like it belonged to him.

The warmth hit his face. The city pulsed with traffic and possibility. For the first time in weeks, maybe months, he felt tall. Not in height. In presence. In purpose.

He didn't check behind him. He didn't fumble for keys. He just walked.

The check was folded neatly in his jacket. But he didn't need to touch it to know it was there.

He felt it in every breath. Every footstep. Every nod from a stranger, a look of respect instead of pity.

He passed a homeless man near the curb. The guy looked up with sunburned cheeks and hollow eyes. Brad didn't stop. He didn't toss coins. He didn't feel the pull to relate. Not anymore.

Not today.

Today, he was someone else.

Today, he had moved on.

# CHAPTER 40

The aroma of popcorn and floor cleaner filled the dorm hallway at Rutgers University, a collage of cheap comfort and quiet anxiety. Brad stood in front of the worn white door, its number plaque askew. He raised his hand and knocked. The sounds of faint music and muffled laughter echoed down the corridor, but the door in front of him opened with caution.

Cassie appeared, nineteen and striking—her jeans cuffed just above worn Converse sneakers, her blond hair pulled into a loose ponytail. Her eyes, the color of bottled honey, widened in suspicion as she looked at the man before her. She was the spitting image of her mother, Cindy, so much so that Brad's breath caught for just a second.

"Who is it?" she asked, arms crossed, defensive.

Brad didn't try to smile. His voice became quiet, sincere. "You don't know me. I knew your mother."

Cassie stared at him, her face unreadable. "What do you want?"

"Can I speak to you, please?"

She hesitated, then stepped back, unlocking the door fully and giving a small, reluctant motion for him to enter. Brad walked inside. The dorm room was tidy, a small single with motivational quotes tacked to a corkboard and a laptop humming on the desk. The scent of vanilla lotion and fresh laundry filled the air.

"I became friends with your mother when I was in Vegas," Brad said, his eyes scanning the room as if it gave him some grounding.

Cassie's gaze dropped to the floor. "Why are you here?"

Brad reached into the inner pocket of his coat. He withdrew a plain envelope and held it out to her. "I have something for you."

Cassie glanced at him. She slid a finger under the flap and peeked inside. Her eyes widened as she pulled out the check, blinking at the figure. "What is this?"

"It's just spending money," Brad said, as if handing out life-altering sums was an everyday thing. "To help with your expenses. I stopped by admissions earlier and paid your tuition. You're covered for the next three years."

She looked up, stunned. "Why are you doing this?"

"Your mother helped me," he said. "In many ways. I'm just paying back the favor."

He turned to leave.

Cassie took a half-step forward. "Thank you," she said, her voice a whisper.

Brad paused and turned to face her again.

"Take care of yourself," he said, extending a hand for a formal goodbye.

It was polite. Distant. The kind of gesture that drew lines in the sand.

But before his fingers could even close around air, Cassie stepped forward—and pulled him into a hug.

Not a casual goodbye embrace. A full-body, no-barriers bear hug. Her arms clung around him like she was afraid he'd dissolve if she let go. Her cheek pressed against his shoulder. Her breath caught in his shirt.

Brad froze.

His first instinct was to step back—to keep it clean. But something about the grip in her arms, the way her fingers curled into the fabric at his back, stopped him. It wasn't seduction. It wasn't even guilt.

It was something simpler. Sadder.

Grief from Cindy's passing. Gratitude for the money.

He closed his eyes and let the moment settle.

"Finish school, make your mother proud."

They stood like that for several seconds, wrapped in silence.

When he pulled away, he did so in a gentle manner, untangling her arms with care rather than force.

Cassie looked up at him, her eyes glassy but dry. "Good luck... back home," she said, her voice steady but softer than usual—almost grateful.

Brad gave a small smile, not smug, not distant. Just human. He didn't answer. Didn't need to.

He nodded once, a silent acknowledgment, not to Cindy's daughter, but to Cindy, and the brief friendship they had shared.

Then he turned and walked to the door.

No rush. No drama. Goodbyes had already been spoken in everything that wasn't said.

Brad reached for the knob, pausing as his fingers touched the cool metal. Behind him, the room fell quiet. No guilt. No longing. Just a faint trace of understanding hanging in the air.

Cassie stayed where she was, listening to the silence settle. She didn't cry. She didn't call after him. She just stood there, her arms folded loosely across her chest.

He stepped into the hallway, dim and ordinary, the way most endings are, letting the door swing shut behind him with a soft click—nothing dramatic, nothing harsh.

Just... final.

# CHAPTER 41

Brad moved through the bright, sterile corridors of North-western Memorial Hospital, a dozen red roses cradled in one arm like a fragile hope. Each step echoed against the polished tile, measured and deliberate—not rushed, but carrying the restless urgency of a man who knew how much he had to make right. The scent of antiseptic clung to the air, clean and cold, but he hardly noticed. All he could think about was her.

At the nurses' station, he paused, his voice quiet but edged with the kind of tension that only love—and regret—can build.

"My wife is Mary Morgan. What room is she in?"

The nurse looked up, her fingers dancing across the keyboard. Her eyes met his with a smile softened by understanding. "Room 504," she said with a nod that felt like a blessing.

"Thank you," Brad whispered, and offered her a grateful smile before continuing down the hallway.

The roses shifted with each step, their scent rich and soft, a romantic contrast to the clinical sterility around him. From the ceiling speakers, as if on cue, the tender notes of Billy Preston's *'You Are So Beautiful'* melody drifted down and poured through the corridor like sunlight, slow and soulful, as though the universe itself had set the stage.

When Brad reached Room 504, his hand hovered on the door for a moment, his heart thudding with a mix of fear and longing. Then, he pushed it open.

What he saw stole the breath from his lungs.

Mary sat upright in the hospital bed, supported by soft pillows, her dark hair a little mussed, her skin pale but luminous in the morning light. In her arms, wrapped in a blue and white blanket, far too big for such a tiny body, their newborn son nursed. The room was hushed, wrapped in the sacred stillness of a new life. Everything else fell away.

Mary looked up. Their eyes met.

For a moment, the world stopped turning.

They didn't speak. They didn't have to. In that gaze, there were no accusations, no regrets—only the full ache and beauty of shared history, and the kind of love that survives the storm.

Brad stepped inside, as if afraid to disturb the spell. He crossed to the bed and without asking, without needing to, eased himself beside her. He placed the roses on the nightstand, petals trembling with the motion. His hand drifted toward the baby, uncertain at first, then steady—his fingers grazing the soft curve of the child's face like a prayer answered.

The baby stirred but didn't cry. Then, with instinctive grace, a tiny hand curled around Brad's finger.

He inhaled, eyes shining. A smile bloomed on his face—not one of pride or triumph, but of awe. Of return. Of something lost being found again.

He turned to Mary, his heart in his throat, and leaned in.

His lips found her forehead in a kiss so soft it barely landed, yet it carried the weight of everything he'd ever wanted to say.

*I'm sorry.      I see you.      I'm here now.*

It wasn't the kind of moment a man walks away from—it stayed, quiet and permanent, mending what had come undone without ever needing to speak.

For a beat, Brad just hovered there, his lips pressed against her skin, letting the silence do what words had always failed to. Her skin was warm, damp from tears that hadn't dried and saturated with the sterile scent of the hospital mingled with her shampoo—something floral, familiar.

She didn't move. But she didn't pull away.

And that was enough.

When he pulled back, Mary's eyes fluttered open. Red-rimmed but steady. She looked up at him, as if trying to confirm that this was real—that he was here, and not just a guilt-shaped shadow passing through.

Brad's throat tightened.

There was so much he wanted to tell her. About the lies. About Vegas. About the money and what it had cost him. About the father he'd lost just moments before finding the part of himself he thought was gone.

But this wasn't the time. Not yet.

Right now, all that mattered was her.

Her and the baby. Their baby.

Mary opened her mouth, like she might speak, but then stopped. Whatever she'd meant to say dissolved behind her lips. She just nodded once, and then her fingers slipped into his—not clinging, not desperate Connected.

Brad sank into the chair beside her, never letting go of her hand. He glanced down at the hospital blanket tucked around her legs, the pale blue wristband, the IV line snaking into her arm. Machines beeped behind them. A gentle rhythm. Like breath. Like hope.

The room wasn't quiet, but it felt still. And in that stillness, Brad exhaled for the first time in what felt like years.

He brought her hand to his lips and kissed her knuckles, slow and reverent. Her hand was trembling, but she didn't pull it away.

They sat like that, side by side, no longer perfect, no longer pretending—but present.

Outside the window, morning had arrived unnoticed. Pale light spilled across the sill like forgiveness made visible.

Brad let it touch his face.

He didn't know what the future held.

But he would be there, by her side, raising their child... together.

# EPILOGUE

*F*ive Years Later

The Morgan home had grown in size and spirit. No longer the modest dwelling that once echoed with quiet fears and late-night whispers, this house exuded warmth, success, and family. Sunlight poured through cathedral windows onto polished hardwood floors. Everything—down to the curated bookshelf, the grand fireplace, and the family photos lining the mantel—spoke of hard-earned peace.

Brad sat in the center of the oversized sectional, his arms wrapped around his wife, Mary, with their five-year-old son, Marcus, nestled between them. The three of them were huddled together under a plush gray blanket, eyes glued to the flat-screen TV that dominated the living room wall. *Man of Steel* played in glorious surround sound, and Marcus—still dressed in his white Karate gi from earlier that afternoon—watched with wide-eyed wonder, chomping on handfuls of buttery popcorn.

Brad leaned toward his son with a dramatic warning. "Watch out, Marcus," he said, his voice low and theatrical. "Superman is coming. Man of Steel rules the day."

He reached down and tickled Marcus under the arms. The boy burst into a stream of laughter, squirming beneath the blanket, his tiny feet kicking out from under it.

Mary leaned in, resting her head on Brad's shoulder. "Marcus wants to show you the move he learned in class today," she whispered with amusement. "He refuses to take off his uniform until he shows you."

Brad smiled and stretched, then stood up with exaggerated seriousness. He crossed his arms and looked down at his son. "Okay, grasshopper," he said in a mock-serious tone. "Let's see what you've learned."

With the ceremony of a miniature martial artist, Marcus leapt off the couch and landed in a sturdy stance, his tiny bare feet gripping the hardwood. He took a moment to compose himself, then demonstrated his new technique: *Choku-zuki*, the straight punch. He jabbed into the air with adorable intensity, repeating the punch over and over as if facing an invisible foe.

Then, giggling, Marcus launched a soft punch at Brad's hip.

Brad reeled back in mock pain. "What am I, a punching bag?"

Marcus beamed. "Daddy, Daddy! You are a bag?"

Brad laughed, tousling his son's hair. "No, Daddy is not a bag," he said, scooping the boy into a bear hug. He spun him once and then plopped him back onto the sofa, where Mary waited with an amused smile.

Snuggling in again, Brad slung his arm around Mary while Marcus flopped down beside them like a tired puppy. The boy reached for the popcorn bowl only to find it empty.

"Mom, I want more popcorn!" Marcus declared, as if this injustice must be immediately addressed.

"You've had enough, Marcus," Mary said. "That was the last box. We're out."

Brad stood, stretching. "I can go to the store," he offered. "I need some 'good juice' from the 'good juice store' anyway."

Mary rolled her eyes but smiled as she leaned back into the couch cushions.

Brad walked over to the side table, picked up his car keys, and made his way to the door. Just as he reached for the handle, Marcus ran over to him.

"Daddy! Daddy! Can I come?" Marcus pleaded, tugging on his pant leg.

Brad crouched down and scooped him up in his arms. He planted a kiss on his son's cheek and smiled.

"No, son," he said. "You can't come with me, but I'll be back. I promise."

He lowered Marcus back to the floor.

Marcus straightened his back, clenched his fists, and executed one final, proud *Choku-zuki*—his tiny face beaming with purpose.

Brad watched for a moment, his heart full, then stepped out the door.

———◆———

He left with the keys in his hand and the sound of his son's laughter still ringing like a hymn in his chest. The front door clicked shut behind him, but the warmth lingered, solid, living, real. Marcus hadn't chased after him, hadn't wrapped his arms around his leg or pleaded for one more story. He hadn't needed to.

Because Brad had said the words his own father never did—*I'll be back.*

And for once, a boy could believe his father.

The road stretched out like a ribbon of forgiveness beneath his tires, quiet and unbroken. The world around him moved with a father tossing a ball to his daughter, a baby pressed close against a mother's chest, a boy learning to ride a bike with laughter stitched into his fear. Ordinary things, yes. But to Brad, they were holy.

For a long time, that kind of life wasn't meant for men like him. Not with the blood he carried. Not with the shadows that followed. His father had vanished behind locked doors and silenced guns, leaving behind questions in drawers and scars in bank vaults. Brad had grown up learning that leaving was inevitable. That fathers disappeared. That men like Logan Morgan didn't say goodbye—they just didn't come back.

The world turned as usual, unaware of the despair inside one small apartment: a boy who had once said, *I don't want toys, I just want my father...*

His father never responded. His son would never have reason to voice those words.

Because he was not his father.

He had walked away from the fire and toward the quiet. He had stood in that hospital room, eyes full of fear and wonder, and knelt beside a life that didn't ask for perfection, just presence. That moment, simple and wordless, had become his redemption.

He told Marcus he was leaving for popcorn and "the good juice," but the truth was heavier and more beautiful. He was delivering a promise. One small enough to live in a child's heart. *I'm yours. I'm here. I'm not going anywhere.*

Because not all fathers leave.

Some return.

Some stay.

And some become the kind of men their son will wait at the window for, not in fear but in faith.

Thank you so much for taking the time to read *Redemption By Default*. I hope you enjoyed it and wouldn't mind leaving a review on Amazon. Every review helps new readers discover my books. Please scan the barcode to leave a review.

If you have enjoyed reading this, you may also enjoy *A Killing at Early Dawn*, my first novel!

# ABOUT THE AUTHOR

**K**athryn McGrady is a Texas native who resides in Central Florida with her husband, Kenneth, her personal and dedicated editor. She is an accomplished author and filmmaker whose creative voice spans multiple genres and formats. Writing both fiction and nonfiction, she explores the emotional weight of relationships, often layered with suspense, psychological depth, and spirituality. Her background in film and storytelling brings a cinematic richness to her work, inviting readers into worlds, some imaginary, some real, where boldness, tension, and transformation collide.

Beyond writing, Kathryn is a visual artist, coloring book creator, and an unapologetic lover of word games. She can often be found behind camera lens, filming, other times immersed in a marathon of gripping television dramas, or locked in a fierce yet friendly game of Scrabble. She believes in the healing power of storytelling and whether crafting a page-turning novel or an empowering self-help guide, Kathryn's voice is bold, honest, and always reaching to entertain, thrill and guide.

To connect with Kathryn

Visit her website: https://www.kathrynmcgrady.com

www.amazon.com/author/kathrynmcgrady

www.instagram/kathrynmcgradybooks

www.tiktok.com/@visionkbooks

www.pinterest.com/visionkbooks

# ALSO BY

---

FICTION

*A Killing at Early Dawn*

*Redemption By Default*

*SinSation*

*Dinner With Lexie (A short story)*

*The Silent Syringe (A short story)*

*The Queen's Quest (A short story)*

*ALL-IN (A short story)*

*The Good Daughter (A short story)*

*Unfinished Business (short film)*

---

NONFICTION

*Letting Him Go When He Cheats*

*The Treasured Coloring Book Collection For Toddlers*